LUCY
AND THE
DJINN

Pranoy Mathew is an Indian-born novelist, designer and photographer, currently residing in Sweden. His debut novel, *Lucy and the Djinn*, is deeply inspired by his own personal experiences with the supernatural, reflecting his lifelong curiosity about things beyond the ordinary. When he's not writing, you'll find Pranoy immersed in exploring the mysteries of the occult and magic, or simply contemplating life's deeper questions.

He loves connecting with readers and is always open to engaging conversations. Find him on Instagram, Facebook, LinkedIn or YouTube @pranoymathew. For updates on his latest works, visit his website at www.pranoymathew.com.

LUCY
AND THE
DJINN

PRANOY MATHEW

Published by Westland Books, a division of Nasadiya Technologies Private Limited, in 2024

No. 269/2B, First Floor, 'Irai Arul', Vimalraj Street, Nethaji Nagar, Alapakkam Main Road, Maduravoyal, Chennai 600095

Westland and the Westland logo are the trademarks of Nasadiya Technologies Private Limited, or its affiliates.

ISBN:

10 9 8 7 6 5 4 3 2 1

Typeset by Mukul

Printed at

*To the forces that brought this story to life, I am grateful for the
imagination you gifted me.
To my mother, for her unwavering support;
my father, for teaching me kindness;
and to Inga, my toughest critic.*

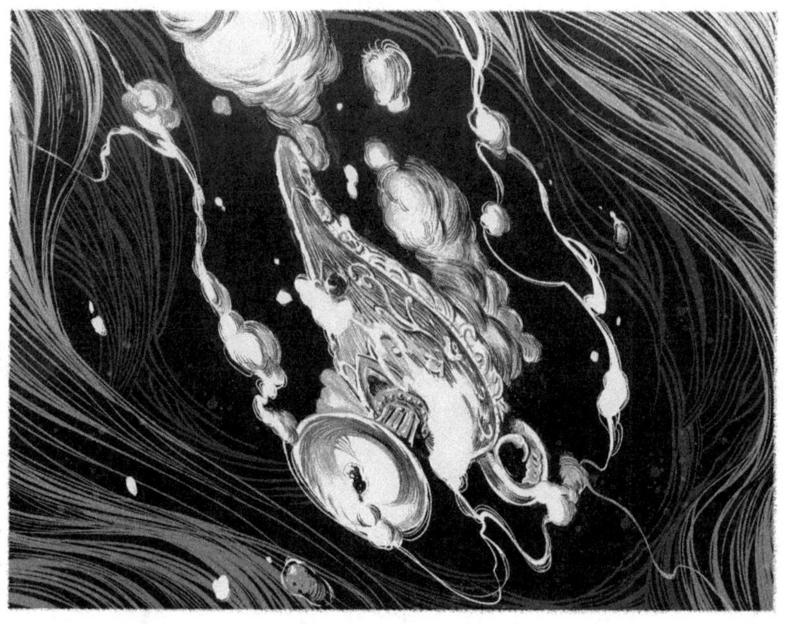

'I have waited for ages, and now you have found me.
Here, our story begins.'

Prologue

'At times, we all need to be saved.'

In the fleeting instant before disaster struck, a sinister tranquillity hung in the air like an unspoken omen. Lucy's eyes were momentarily drawn to the blood smeared across her dress, a macabre canvas of crimson stains echoing the chaotic brushstrokes of a tormented artist. A chilling memory surged to the forefront of her thoughts—Paul's skull fracturing with a nauseating crunch, his agonised screams spiralling into a nightmarish, guttural cacophony that reverberated through the darkest corners of her soul.

Snapping out of the chilling memory, Lucy gripped the steering wheel tightly, her knuckles turning white. She looked at the rain-slicked road ahead, a treacherous labyrinth of serpentine bends swallowed by the inky void of the night. A shroud of mystery enveloped the path as fog slithered in like a vengeful wraith, the solitary streetlight's feeble glow flickering in a futile battle against the encroaching darkness. Ominous shadows pirouetted through the relentless downpour as if taunting her with each movement.

Driven by an insatiable need to escape the torment of her own demons, Lucy's foot slammed down on the accelerator, the sudden surge of power causing the speedometer needle to race skyward. The world outside blurred into a maelstrom of chaos and speed, her heart pounding in beat with the thundering engine as she hurtled headlong into the unknown.

Without warning, Uncle George's face flickered onto the car's screen, an unexpected incoming call that momentarily snatched her focus. In the split second Lucy's gaze drifted from the road, fate struck with a merciless hand. A deafening chorus of rending metal and shattering glass erupted, heralding the cataclysmic collision that would alter the course of her life.

The airbags detonated with ferocious force, their explosive impact shattering Lucy's nose and hurling her violently against the seat. Above the din of destruction, the tortured wail of screeching tyres pierced the air, a haunting testament to the chaos unfolding around her. Abruptly, Lucy was engulfed by a disorienting sensation of weightlessness. Her car, now an unwilling participant in a gravity-defying dance, twisted and somersaulted through the air. The chaos of the moment seemed to stretch time itself, each second elongating into eternity.

As Lucy hung suspended in the disorienting void, her gaze became fixated on the levitating bottles of Jack Daniel's, their amber contents swirling into miniature tempests within the confines of their glass prisons. Time seemed to stand still just before the gut-wrenching crunch of impact, as the car met its watery demise, nosediving into the depths of Lake Bhujanga Dasayya.

Inverted and engulfed by the dark water, the mangled wreckage commenced its descent, a grotesque, twisted metal tomb surrendering to the cold, murky embrace of the abyss below. The initial impact had momentarily knocked Lucy unconscious, but the numbing chill of the water jolted her back to awareness. Her breaths came in ragged, panicked gasps, her lungs screaming for air as the icy water continued to fill the mangled car.

As the water level crept higher, submerging her chest and then her neck, she fought desperately against the crushing weight of the seatbelt, her fingers clawing at the release button. With a final, desperate surge of adrenaline, Lucy managed to free herself from the seatbelt's death grip, but the darkness had already begun to encroach upon the edges of her vision. The car, now a sinking spectre, continued its plunge into the depth, vanishing into the stygian void of the lake.

Burdened by exhaustion, Lucy persisted in her struggle to escape the doomed vehicle. Her final breath slipped from her lips, a silvery bubble ascending into the gloom. The slowing rhythm of her heart provided a sombre soundtrack to the cascade of memories flooding her consciousness—her parents' tragic demise, Zacharia, her bouts of paranoia, and the bittersweet dance of finding and losing love. Each memory played out in vivid detail, a poignant reminder of the life that had led her to this very moment.

In the throes of desperation, as the darkness threatened to consume her entirely, a glimmer of hope flickered within her mind. She recalled the ancient lamp and the formidable being it sheltered. With the last vestiges of her strength, she mustered a desperate cry for deliverance: *Iblis, I need help! I am dying! Please, help me!*

Above the water's surface, a resplendent light burst forth, spreading like a relentless inferno. It penetrated the dark depths, casting aside the shadows as if night had been vanquished by the arrival of the day. Within the luminous radiance, a gargantuan figure materialised, descending with an air of determination. The being possessed three heads—one of a bull, another of a snake, and the last of a man—and each fixed upon Lucy as it swam in her direction.

1

Death. Why does it always have to come at the wrong time? Lucy pondered as she sat in the taxi from the airport to the funeral.

Outside, the road from Nedumbassery to Vaitila was lined with political campaigns for the upcoming 2014 general election. Grown men sporting amusing moustaches stood pleasantly with their hands clasped in the posters, promising a secure future for Kerala and the country in the coming years. Lucy observed their overly polite gestures to keep her mind distracted. In all honesty, her faith in these politicians and the system they represented had evaporated long before she reached voting age eight years ago. It wasn't that she harboured a deep disdain for democracy or rejected the idea that everything would ultimately work out. Rather, it was difficult to reconcile such notions with her own experiences, which had been far from idyllic for so long. She wondered where people even got the idea of things going so well—in what world does that happen?

Even before reaching her destination, the scent of incense began to fill her thoughts—the way the kapiare (priest's helper) would always stand next to the coffin, seemingly intent on suffocating everyone in the room with the thick, fragrant smoke. The smell of incense brought back memories of her parents who had tragically died in an accident in Ooty when she was just a young girl. At their funeral too, there had been a kapiare diligently tending to the slow-burning aroma of pure frankincense, the scent forever etched in her memory.

You see, odours can trigger more vivid and emotionally charged memories. It is true. They call it the Proustian effect or something, after some French author.

The faces of her parents flickered in Lucy's mind. They lacked details, almost like an old black and white photograph from a bygone era. Another distant memory waiting to be forgotten. She retrieved an already opened bottle of Jack Daniel's from her duty-free bag and took a generous swig. The driver looked in the rear-view mirror and passed a dirty glance.

'Are you okay, madam?'

'Yeah, I'm fine. Just look straight and drive.'

'It's not common for my passengers to drink, madam. The owner of this car is very strict about this sort of thing—I might lose my job if he finds out.'

'Just look straight and drive.'

'If you want, I can stop at a hotel and wait for you, meter charge only.'

'That won't be necessary. I don't have to go far. But thank you!'

The driver shifted gears harshly in protest and pressed on the accelerator.

On the street outside Palathikal House, white cars with red VIP licence plates were parked closely together, indicating the arrival of ministers, police chiefs, businessmen, and media personnel—the usual suspects. There were also neighbours, employees, local party members and churchgoers, all vying for limited space. And to make things worse, the funeral had begun thirty minutes before and the crowd, with their umbrellas open from the sun, resembled a pack of demons waiting for her arrival. Her hands started trembling, the usual morning tremors.

'Are you from the Palathikal family? I didn't know, madam. Sorry,' the driver said, keeping his eyes down as he finally dropped her off in front of the huge white mansion. Lucy didn't reply; instead, she tossed a few five hundred rupee notes onto the front seat and jumped out of the car.

Usually, Lucy avoided crowds. She felt they judged her harshly and made her feel obnoxious for no reason. The very idea of walking into those strangers caused her face to flush and feet to sweat. But there was no other way to get to her grandfather. On her course to the casket, Lucy saw the vacant dog shelter where her German Shepherd Tipu used to reside. Next to it stood the dying Alphonso mango tree, the one she used to climb as a young girl. Her home had changed a lot, yet remnants of its past still lingered in the form of stubborn, unchanging objects.

Father Kurian's prayers blasted through the speakers under the blue tarpaulin tent where the coffin was placed in the central stage. As usual, the older priest was enthusiastic about the blessed soul finding its way to heaven.

Lucy's gaze swept across the space, finally resting on her aunts, uncles and other relatives who occupied the front row, next to the many funeral wreaths with name tags. Despite the distance, she could discern the signs of ageing etched onto their faces—deep wrinkles and strands of grey hair that spoke of the inexorable march of time.

Although she was not endowed with the gift of mind-reading, Lucy could sense that her relatives were all consumed with the contents of August Zacharia's last will and testament. *How can they not?* Afterall, his vast empire included estates, tea plantations, seafood factories, hotels. Not to forget his crown jewel—the *Daily Malayalam*.

'Ayyo, see that young, spoilt brat, huh?' 'No respect for the dead, I swear.' 'Don't know why she even bothered to come here.' Lucy could hear the crowd murmuring—almost. Lucy could hear them—almost. They all wanted her to fail. They wanted her to go back. Her thin hands started shaking, and her legs started wobbling. Her anxiety became overwhelming—she immediately grabbed the bottle from the bag. She took a swig—again.

'Lucy molae, don't be afraid, this is your home. Allae? I am happy you are back,' someone whispered in her ears, a familiar voice.

'Appappa, I don't feel that I belong here. Maybe I should leave before someone notices me.'

'Don't you want to give me one final kiss before they lay me to rest in our family cemetery?'

'Yes, Appappa, I do.'

'Then come and sit close to me, next to my casket.'

Jancy chechi, the sixty-year-old housekeeper, was keeping a watchful eye on the crowd when she spotted Lucy from afar. Despite the distance, Jancy could see the discomfort carved on the young girl's face. Without a moment's hesitation, she raised her hand and called out, 'Molae, over here!' and quickly made her way towards Lucy to offer her assistance.

'Look, who's here! I almost didn't recognise you! I heard you weren't going to come to Acchayan's ceremony,' the older woman said as she firmly took hold of Lucy's wrist and led her through the crowd. 'Did you eat anything on the way here? We have appam and vegetable stew in the kitchen. Come with me, you must be tired from all the travelling.'

Jancy chechi. What a relief. Thank God!

Lucy followed the older women to the kitchen in an attempt to set foot into the ancestral house without grabbing much attention. On her way, Appapan from the casket asked again: 'Where is my final kiss?' But she kept her face away.

The insides of Palathikal House were filled with a mix of familiar and unfamiliar faces. Some smiled while others frowned. Her old schoolteachers, neighbours, maids and cousins were all present, and she could sense their questions without them even saying a word: 'Where had she vanish all these years, eh? Heard she's going through a divorce or something. Just look at her, all worn out and weak.'

Jancy chechi picked up a porcelain plate from the shelf and filled it with a few fluffy appams, generously ladled with homemade vegetable stew. Though she pretended to be uninterested, Lucy's stomach let out a growl of hunger.

And as the young woman munched her way into her late lunch, Jancy chechi attempted to make conversation about her short, coloured hair and multiple piercings on the left ear.

'Remember when we used to sit on the veranda and comb your long hair together? We used to oil it with Neelabrigathi Thailam. It used to be very ...' chechi continued. Lucy passed an *I am not interested* nod.

Why do old people always dwell on the past? It's as if they can't let it go. Does reminiscing about their past provide them with a false sense of security?

'Did it hurt when they put all that in your left ear? I hear when you put piercings over there, it takes some time to heal, and you also have it on your eyebrows. Is it a city style?' Jancy chechi continued. Lucy moved her face closer to the plate.

'Did Appapan tell you anything about the will? Do you think he mentioned me in it?' Lucy muttered as she chewed on the potato. Yesterday, when she received a call from the lawyer, that was the first thing he mentioned over the phone—that there was a package waiting for her and it was important for her to be present at home to receive it.

'Molae, Zacharia sir was very silent the past few years, always in his room going through the old albums. A week before he passed away, he was asking if you were around and when I told him you live in Bangalore now, he got very angry. Alzheimer's, you know, very unpredictable.' Jancy chechi kept both her knuckles under her jaw and passed a sad gasp.

I hope he left behind enough to pay back my debts, Lucy thought.

2

It is said that when Lucy's great-grandfather Cheriyan took his life at the age of forty-five, the only thing left behind was massive debt.

Zacharia was fifteen years old then—a scrawny chap with an unpleasant smile. His older brothers, overwhelmed by newfound responsibilities, escaped to Bombay, abandoning their mother and younger sister to fend off local predators. When the thugs arrived, claiming they had lent money to Cheriyan and taunting that Zacharia's mother and sister could repay the debt with their bodies, the teenager dropped off school early to find employment.

His first job was assisting a local fish merchant in Chambakkara Market. He unloaded the fish from the boats and displayed them in the open stand, bellowing with gusto: 'Meene venno, Meen. Fresh fish. Best fish. Ayilla Matti, Chura. Meene venno Meene.' When someone made a purchase, he expertly gutted the fish, removed its entrails and chopped it into curry-sized portions, ultimately wrapping them in banyan leaves.

During those years, he woke up before dawn and returned home only after midnight, labouring until he collapsed without ever complaining. Within a few years, on his eighteenth birthday, the boy who had once been deemed useless opened a seafood wholesale shop with the help of his employer.

A small board was soon put up: Palathikal Seafood Co.

Seven decades later, the boy had amassed a fortune greater than the former rulers of Cochin. In addition to owning hundreds of fishing vessels throughout the Arabian Sea, he also possessed a multitude of seafood restaurants and resorts. There was also the textile import business from Europe and the Middle East, a food processing company called Ilachi and a film studio in Madras. The list had no end. But out of all his gems, the one that stood out the most was the *Daily Malayalam,* a newspaper agency that became a staple for thirty-four million Malayalees since the 1960s. It was rumoured that in his prime Zacharia held considerable sway in Kerala politics and had a monopoly in publishing.

But nobody, not even his mother, was aware of how his circumstances transformed so dramatically—how an individual who had scarcely completed high school ascended to the position of CEO of an empire.

Some who witnessed his rise tried to spread rumours that he was involved with narcotics—that Zacharia had connections with the mafia and helped them import contraband through Kochi port. Others believed he had delved into durmathravadam (witchcraft) and paid obeisance to a kuttichattan (devil), a very prevalent practice that survived generations in Kerala.

But those who were close to him believed the man possessed a sharp knack for trade. They held him in high esteem as a savvy entrepreneur who fearlessly fought for the rights of the common man. Despite the conflicting notion of who he was, everyone agreed that Zacharia had an extraordinary talent to foresee the future. It was like he had a fortune teller's crystal ball and knew how to use it.

After the birth of his three children from a late marriage, Zacharia slowly began to reside in the comforts of his home. He kept a firm grip on his companies and local politics but spent most of his time mentoring his younger ones to take over his empire.

His oldest son, George, was smart and cunning, ruthless in his endeavours even as a teenager. And for that, his father treated him differently and gave him responsibilities early in life. In business, Zacharia knew, it is only people like George who survive.

His only daughter, Elza, had her own ways of making sure she emerged victorious in every game she played. She knew how people worked and used it to her advantage. Determined and driven, she pursued her desires relentlessly.

And though Zacharia tried to see all his children as equals, like all other parents he had a favourite—his youngest son, David, the kindest of them all.

When both his elder siblings were sent abroad for studies, David was kept at a hand's distance. It might be this sort of kind nature that led him to marry early and eventually produce the first heir to the family, Lucy. Ever since then, Lucy had been in Zacharia's thoughts. His first granddaughter, his favourite, the one he truly cared about. Though everyone enjoyed David and his wife's soothing company, fate had another plan for them. Their untimely death was a blow to the family. Zacharia was never the same after that.

In his old age, Zacharia often communicated with others in a cryptic tone. He mentioned many times that he could talk to the dead and could hear other people's thoughts. Many, including his children, took it as a sign of the old man losing his mind, blaming it on the Alzheimer's that nibbled on his brain cells.

Hours before his death, the old man revealed to his lawyer that his last will was not just a transfer of wealth but also a message from the dead to the ones who still roam in this world. And its reasons would only be revealed in time.

3

The church brimmed with the faithful. Before the cross bearing the weight of Jesus, the priest offered his prayers to the heavens. At his feet lay an open casket, within which Zacharia rested in eternal slumber, a picture of serenity.

Thoughts of how the old man's wealth would be divided made churchgoers' bottoms tickle. They were like circus animals in a cage waiting for the day's meal. To God, they prayed for forgiveness, for the greed and jealousy that swelled in their hearts. As soon as the Mass concluded at Vallarpadam Basilica, and the casket was lowered to the ground, cars promptly departed for Palathikal House.

Upon returning to the three-storey concrete bungalow, Boban, the lawyer, instructed them to take a seat in the main hall on chairs bearing their respective names.

In the foremost row of pews, Maria—Zacharia's second wife, a fifty-year-old widow—sat beside her fourteen-year-old son, Alvin. Just behind them, George—Zacharia's firstborn from his first marriage—settled in with his wife, Gracy, and their twenty-year-old twins, Janet and Jackson.

Elza, Zacharia's daughter, occupied the next row with her husband, a heart surgeon from the USA. Seats, though vacant, bore the names of Lucy's late parents, David and Caroline. On the periphery of that row, Lucy shared the space with a smattering of distant cousins and other relatives.

Feeling the unease and apprehension in the room, Boban retrieved the sealed envelope from his aged leather satchel. In the hush that followed, everyone held their breath, hoping for a stroke of luck to grace upon them.

Last Will and Testament of August Zacharia

I, **AUGUST ZACHARIA**, a resident of Kochi, Kerala, and a citizen of India, being of full age, sound mind, memory and understanding, do hereby make, publish and declare this to be my Last Will and Testament, hereby revoking all Last Wills and Testaments and Codicils there to attached, here to fore made by me. In this Will, I express, as I did many times during my life, my love, affection and admiration for my late first wife Susanna Zacharia. I direct that I be interred wearing both my gold wedding rings (which are never to be removed from my finger) and that my remains be interred next to my beloved late wife.

Article One: Bequests

A. I direct that all my just debts, funeral expenses, last illness expenses, if any, and the cost of administration of my belonging be paid out of the assets of my belongings as soon after my demise as may be practicable. Such debts shall not include obligations secured by mortgages on real property and loans secured by a cooperative apartment.

B. I direct my executors to sell all my residences and properties that I may own at my death except 'Palathikal House' and to add the net proceeds of the sale to the charity organisation that I managed with my late first wife Susanna Zacharia (Referred to within this document as the 'Trust').

C. I direct my executors to sell all my furniture, furnishings, books, paintings and other objects of art, wearing apparel, jewellery, automobiles and all other tangible personal property, and the money from the sale should be given equally to everyone gathered at my funeral.

D. I direct that the following bequests be made in trust for each of the following persons. I intend that each of them will receive a flow of 'income' as defined in the Trust and (except as expressly provided) after each person dies, the trust assets will pass to the charity organisations that were managed by Susanna Zacharia before her death.

(1) If my second wife **MARIA ZACHARIA** survives me, I leave the sum of Ten Crore rupees (₹10,00,00,000) to the trust established for her benefit under paragraph **A** of Article **FOUR**.

(2) If my youngest son **ALVIN ZACHARIA** survives me, I leave the sum of Five Crore rupees (₹5,00,00,000) to the trust established for his benefit under paragraph **B** of Article **FOUR**.

(3) If my oldest son **GEORGE ZACHARIA** survives me, I leave him all my shares in Daily Malayalam and its subsidiaries. He won't be able to sell/transfer this to anyone else outside the direct family, and after his death, all the shares go to the family Trust.

(4) If my only daughter **ELZA ZACHARIA** survives me, I leave her all my shares in Daily Hotels and its subsidiaries. She won't be able to sell/transfer this to anyone else outside the direct family, and after her death, all the shares go to the family Trust.

(5) If my granddaughter **LUCY DAVID** survives me, I leave her the key to my safe (referred to within this document as

the 'Trust'). All objects in the safe belong to her and after her death should be thrown into the Arabian Sea.

(6) If my housekeeper **JANCY CHERIYAN** survives me, I leave her the ownership of Palathikal House and the three acres of land surrounding it.

Before Boban could finish reading, loud clamours erupted from the gathered crowd. Some expressed joy while others sadness. Some murmured to themselves while others praised God. Among the happy ones was George Zacharia who got the lion's share of his father's fortune. And then there was Mariamma (as they call her), Zacharia's second wife, who cried and cursed the dead man for not caring enough. Some of the relatives were pleased to receive an amount for just being there and others reminded the lawyer about how close they were to the dead man.

There were also wide objections to giving the ancestral home to Jancy chechi. They pointed out she was not related by blood and had no right to anything. They implored her to return the possession to its rightful owners, and she acquiesced with a disquieted inclination of her head.

Why must she return what was given to her? These greedy bastards! Lucy rose from her seat, her heart racing from the cries and screams. As those initial thoughts ebbed, another wave of contemplation surged: 'Key to a safe? Just a safe? Does that imply I have no claim to his other things?' Panic gripped her as she envisioned a modest safe tucked away in an antiquated bank, containing nothing but a note that read: 'You should have visited me more often, you are ungrateful …'

Lucy felt an odd twinge of guilt for entertaining such thoughts on the very day Zacharia's body found its final resting place. She pictured her grandfather gazing down from the heavens, judging the unruly conduct of the mourners. Yet, she reassured herself, this was not a rarity; people often traverse convoluted and emotionally charged circumstances in ways that defy logic.

She recognised the situation as a case of moral disengagement—a mechanism allowing individuals to distance themselves from their own ethical standards, thus rationalising behaviour they would normally consider immoral or unethical.

Still, even amidst her valiant struggle to untangle the complex web of her emotions, a lingering sense of injustice cast its melancholic shadow upon Lucy's thoughts.

Lucy made her way to the kitchen, where Zacharia habitually stored his liquor. She swung open the cabinet, selected a bottle and filled a glass. Raising it towards the celestial expanse, she toasted, 'Cheers to you, Appappa.'

But the alcohol failed to temper her emotions; instead, it subtly unwound the tightly bound knot of negativity in her mind, sending anxious thoughts whirling in an endless gyre. The image of Jancy chechi, standing defenceless in front of a greedy crowd, replayed on a ceaseless loop. Her uneasy grin and gaze tethered to the ground. *Why must the weak be preyed upon? Why is kindness perceived as frailty?*

Lucy's phone started vibrating. Notifications, emails and WhatsApp messages—a lot were due.

With a sense of dread, she checked her State Bank of India account once more, only to confirm that it was still below the minimum balance. Were it not for the credit card, her fate would have been sealed long ago. *Who would have thought love could be such an exorbitant affair?* she jestingly mused to take the edge of her guilt. *Appapan must have left me something of value. Maybe documents to a secret estate, a suitcase filled with gold, a foreign bank account with millions of dollars.* Lucy tried to imagine all the different things a bank safe could hold.

'They would return, one day.'

Fourteen years ago, when news of the horrific accident reached Palathikal House, Lucy was sleeping on her grandparents' bed.

The twelve-year-old rested calmly on the side of the mattress, hugging her favourite toy and having her usual dreams.

For most of the evening, she complained about her parents' broken promise to call her. If she hadn't played in the rain with Tipu, the four-month-old German Shepherd pup, and fallen ill, she could have accompanied her parents to Ooty. Before getting into their Gypsy, David and Caroline kissed Lucy goodbye. 'We will be back before you know. Stay with Appapan and Ammama till then,' they told her. And that was the last time she saw their faces.

The first person to head to the hospital was Zacharia with his driver, Paulose. They spent the entire next day searching for the hospital around Mettupalayam. And when they arrived, they were immediately asked to verify a bracelet attached to a dismembered hand and a pair of shoes covered in blood—the only recognisable remains of the accident, according to the police.

The rescue team informed Zacharia that the incident might have occurred when David was trying to overtake a truck on one of the hairpin curves. They took the old man to the spot where the car broke the steel fence and fell into the gorge. For the next three months, Zacharia fell into wordless solitude. He upheld a delicate illusion of normalcy, placing two extra plates on the dinner table, as if nothing had happened.

During the funeral, Lucy did not cry or complain. She sat on her grandmother's lap and stared at Father Kurian who administered the last rites to the closed caskets. She was curious about the contents and persistently inquired with the onlookers. However, nobody had the courage to inform her that they contained her parents' ravaged remains.

Instead, they comforted her by placing their hands on her head. They said, in one united feeling: *When the call from the heavens arrives in people's ears, they must leave, that is how it is supposed to be. That is how it has always been.*

Despite the seriousness of the occasion, little Lucy was too young to fully comprehend death. To her, the cycle of life was all the same, just another moment in time that would give way to the future.

Over the next two years, Lucy spent her time sitting by the large window next to Tipu's cage. She remained patient, eagerly anticipating the return of her parents. On some days, she ate and slept next to the cage, oblivious to the truth. Days turned to weeks, weeks to months, but no familiar faces crossed the gate. Lucy held tightly to her enduring hope.

When the family had their evening prayers, where Zakaria, Susanne and Jancy chechi kneeled before the man-sized Jesus statue, she prayed for her parents' return: 'Oh Father up in heaven, hear my prayer, bring back my parents, before the memory of me fades from their hearts.'

She even tried to bribe God by singing his songs louder and making signs of the cross whenever possible. Nothing is impossible to God, and in time he would bring them back, she believed.

In school, Lucy's quiet demeanour rendered her a conspicuous figure, her silence drawing the gaze of her peers. Isolated in her corner of the classroom, she met the stares of onlookers with her own. Her slender height and cropped hair made her an easy target for boisterous boys seeking vulnerable victims. They taunted her with jeers and mocked her sharp nose and manly walk. 'Aanne-Penne, Aanne-Penne. Here comes Anne-Penne,' they chanted each morning as she entered the classroom. 'Anne-Penne' was a colloquialism wielded to deride transgender youth. Lucy knew what it meant but she felt too tired to protest.

After school, Paulose would pick her up in her Appapan's old Jeep. He always had the radio on with new Malayalam music. Some days, Zacharia and Tipu joined too. They went to Cherai to get roasted peanuts and watch the waves crash on the beach.

And Lucy knew from her very first time there that it was one of those spots where people came to forget their everyday problems. Young men and women sat closely and even held hands, as if they were on foreign shores and no agitated crowd would catch them in the act.

As a young girl, Lucy used to observe them with a sense of awe, captivated by the enchanting nature of human connection. There was something tempting about being close to somebody. While she couldn't articulate those emotions, they stirred deeply within her core. She, too, yearned for someone to love and care for.

At home, Susanna, her grandmother always welcomed her with open arms. Together they would converse like grown-ups over tea in the garden. They would gossip about teachers and friends like sisters born in different eras. Tipu would always be around—snipping and barking, trying to lure Lucy to play with him. Before dinner, they would run around the trees, attempting to catch the squirrels who came for the Alphonso mangoes. Then eventually there would be Jancy chechi's loud call—'Molae. Lucy molae. Where are you? Come, have supper. Everyone is waiting'—and Lucy would run to the dining table and Tipu to his cage.

Despite living a simple and carefree life, everything changed for Lucy when she turned fifteen. No one would forget that day she ran into her grandfather's study and set fire to his table, the way she mindlessly screamed at Jancy chechi and her grandparents with a knife on her hand. 'All of you killed my

Appa. You killed Amma. You took me for a fool!' she repeated, holding her left arm up in the air and threatening to harm herself by slitting her wrist.

Afterwards, she confided in Zacharia that she had no recollection of the incident. In her words, those moments were just 'a hazy blur'. It always started with an unexplainable feeling of rage and euphoria before her senses went blank. During those months, she lacked energy, she was always in bed, sad and hopeless, dangerously irritable and constantly complaining about not being able to concentrate or remember things. Some days she did not sleep or eat, wandering around like a zombie in her long white gown.

As manic episodes became more frequent, Zacharia reached out to Dr Kurup, their family physician. And it didn't take long for him to recognise that Lucy was exhibiting early symptoms of schizophrenia, a severe mental illness that made her delusional and unpredictable. The doctor informed the family that the condition might have emerged from her unresolved trauma, and the only way forward was to medicate her heavily.

Over the next three years, Lucy refrained from attending school. Instead, she remained at home, mostly in her room, keeping watch at the gate for her parents' return. The antidepressants did calm her down but they made her dizzy. She complained about being sleepy and exhausted all the time. Her face lost its innocence as dark circles formed around her eyes. She gained a lot of weight and her hair started shedding.

In hindsight, Lucy would only recall this period as fragments of her imagination. An epoch where she was trapped in the limbo of her own mind—a place of dark grim silence.

5

Upon turning nineteen, Lucy's sickness had begun to wane. She slowly regained a portion of her lost self and started behaving with reason.

The new Lucy indulged herself by painting day and night. She drew everything from the dark and desolate to the beautiful and serene. Painting became such an obsession that she had to be dragged out of her room for breakfast and dinner, and even then her mind remained fixated on her art. When Susanna realised how much her granddaughter liked to paint, she employed a retired art teacher named Rajeevan to instruct her in the finer points of the craft.

In the span of just over a year, Lucy produced around a hundred breathtaking paintings, drawing inspiration from the works of modern masters such as Picasso, Monet and Van Gogh. Her artistic creations were not only beautiful but they also conveyed a unique depth of emotion and thought that transcended her years.

Rajeevan was thoroughly impressed. He kept his glasses on and moved his eyes through the fine details of every stroke, marvelling at the intricate textures and vivid colours that Lucy had masterfully blended. 'Lucy, this is truly incredible. You are blessed by Goddess Saraswati,' he often commented. However, he questioned Lucy's fixation on painting the same enigmatic figure: a towering, broad man with three faces.

'What is the meaning of these faces, the serpent, the bull and the man? Is there something specific you're trying to convey?'

'Sir, I'm not entirely certain what I want to achieve with it. Some days I feel I am just a tool for the universe's creations to come alive on a canvas—I barely have control over my own art. I wonder if the man is a symbol of a memory I can't quite remember, a connection from a past life, like we were long-lost companions from another time and place,' Lucy would murmur back. 'Some nights, I sit beneath his piercing gaze, lost in thought, wondering about the stranger's identity and what he might be seeking from me.'

Although Rajeevan was consistently astonished by such responses from the young artist, he chose to view them as signs of genius rather than madness. He was the first one to suggest to her grandparents that Lucy be sent away for further studies. That would allow her blossoming mind to fully flourish.

In the ensuing months, Lucy, with the help of her teacher, convinced both Zacharia and Susanna to allow her to pursue a course in Fine Arts at Banaras Hindu University in Varanasi. She told them that art has become her passion and without it she would suffocate to death.

Many of her relatives, particularly her eldest uncle, George, showed concern. He, along with several others, cautioned Zacharia that sending Lucy away from home while she was still on medication would be a grave mistake. But when the old man looked into his grandchild's innocent eyes, all that he could see was an unquenching thirst to know more about the world. Despite their reservations, Zacharia ultimately agreed to Lucy's requests and made plans to send her to Varanasi.

And that was the last time Zacharia saw Lucy.

6

Bank manager Koshi led the way with broad strides and Lucy followed him. She couldn't help but notice his overly protruding belly that strained against his tight white shirt. She whimsically pictured him devouring a generous portion of chicken biryani, the morsels tumbling from his lips in a curious blend of sadism and anxiety. The thought elicited a giggle from her.

In Koshi's broad hands were signed papers of Zacharia's will that Boban had handed over that morning. They walked past the semi-rusted desks and the small glass cabins towards the inner chambers of Federal Bank.

After crossing the human-sized metal vault and two steel doors, they stopped in front of many numbered steel boxes with tiny keyholes. The metallic scent of enclosed spaces evoked memories of exotic goods some people had once brought for Lucy's grandfather from Persia. Anticipation swelled within her as she pondered the treasures that awaited.

'These are our premium safe vaults, madam,' Koshi explained as he deftly unlocked Safe 26. The door creaked as it opened. From within the compact space, he retrieved a box the size of a cabin bag. A 'Handle with Care' sticker in bold, italicised font was placed on top of it. After handing it over to Lucy, the manager politely requested her signature to complete the transaction.

'Madam, Zacharia sir was one of our most valued customers. I've known him since I first joined this branch as a clerk twenty-five years ago,' Koshi said in a gentle voice. 'It was such a tragedy to hear of his passing. Please accept my condolences.'

'Hmm,' Lucy nodded, still wondering about the contents of the box.

'Sir had kept all his fixed deposits with us for many years, making him our largest single account holder. Last December, he invited me and my family to a Christmas dinner at his house and requested that I open a high-security vault for him, one that would not be recorded in our books.'

Whatever, man! Not interested. Can I just leave? Lucy's countenance shifted into one of tedium, her eyes drifting aimlessly around the room.

'Sir specifically instructed me to remind whoever collected the box that it should not be opened until you reach a safe place. This is very important,' Koshi said with a hint of concern. 'No matter who asks you to open it, you must not do so until you are in a secure location—that is what he said.'

Lucy brushed off the warnings, gave him her final goodbyes and strolled straight to the exit. Beyond the doors, she caught sight of Boban patiently awaiting in his car for her. He gestured towards the back seat, and Lucy hopped in. The old Volkswagen Beetle sputtered to life after a moment of hesitation and Boban shifted the gears roughly before stepping on the accelerator.

Outside, the Monday morning rush was visible—it was a frenetic scene of commuters dashing to their offices, children hurrying off to school and an array of vehicles of every make and model clogging the roads.

Lucy examined the box, delicately running her fingertips over its surface. It was not heavy but neither was it light. It was sealed strenuously on all sides with tapes and stickers. *Must be some rare piece of jewellery,* Lucy speculated, considering Zacharia's penchant for collecting one-of-a-kind antiques.

She recalled that his study boasted a vast collection of valuable pieces sourced from various parts of Asia and Europe, acquired either through international auctions or his journeys during the summer months. Lucy's mind drifted back to her childhood, when she would run through Zacharia's grand room and marvel at the museum-like display cases where rare and exotic artefacts were elegantly arranged—the colourful masks from Africa, intricately carved wooden statues from South Asia and delicate porcelain figurines from China.

'What do you think it is?' she asked Boban.

'What's there to think about?'

'This.' Lucy raised the box up from behind.

'Oh, that, I don't know, molae,' replied Boban with a grin.

He is lying, he knows. A low voice uttered in her ears.

'What?' Lucy moved her head around.

Look into his eyes, you will see it too, the whisper continued.

Lucy stole a quick glance at Boban through the rearview mirror and felt a chill run down her spine. His eyes, usually so calm and collected, now seemed to hold a glint of something sinister. It was as if she could sense the danger lurking just beneath the surface, waiting to pounce at the right moment. Despite her best efforts to shake off the feeling, it persisted, gnawing at her insides like an insistent itch.

'But if you are so eager to know what is inside, why not open it now? We can both have a look,' Boban said as he turned around to look at her.

Keep it closed, keep it closed, it is not safe, an ominous voice reverberated through the car. Without a second thought, she clutched the box closer to her chest.

'Maybe later, I'm too tired to care about it right now.' Lucy kept her eyes on the road. *What was that? What was that voice?*

'Then it's fine. Just gimme a call if it's somethin' interestin',' he replied, pretending to not care. 'Alla, molae, how is life in Bangalore? Is it cold?'

'It is okay, uncle, too crowded to live. I am thinking of moving.'

'How's your start-up doin'? That app or somethin' you were workin' on? Making any money?'

'Aaaa, that's all right. It's going well. User growth is doubling every quarter. We have a big launch coming up in Mumbai.'

'Oh, Mumbai,' Boban's eyes widened in surprise. 'Zacharia sir always used to say that Lucy would go places. But what was it again? Buyin' and sellin' handicrafts or somethin', right?'

'No, no, Boban Uncle, "Picasso" is not about buying and selling handicrafts. It's an app, mobile application, more like a marketplace for local artists. They can sell their paintings to international museums and collectors. And then there is the social network on top of it, so they get the right publicity,' Lucy explained

'Very interestin', molae. Not like my borin' job, sortin' out family partitions and legal disputes between siblings. How's Adityan? Are ya plannin' on havin' children?' Boban asked, sneaking a glance at her through the rearview mirror.

'Adityan is doing fine,' she paused, struggling to find the right words. 'But we are not together anymore.'

'Separated? Already?'

'I haven't signed the papers yet.' Lucy took a deep breath, trying to hold back the overwhelming emotions and anxiety that threatened to consume her. Her hands started shaking, betraying her attempts to appear composed.

'George told me you needed financial help. Is it true? The whole town is talking about it,' Boban's voice carried a hint of gossip. 'And I also heard rumours that Adityan has another wife in Mumbai. Is that true?'

The young woman sat with her arms tightly crossed, refusing to answer. But Boban persisted. 'How does this affect your position in the company? Have you discussed a settlement? And who is representing you in court?' He shook his head disapprovingly. 'Aaaah, you shouldn't have married an outsider. Zacharia sir always said this would happen.'

'Uncle, I am little tired. I need to close my eyes for some time.'

'See, molae, this is not something to close your eyes to. You must negotiate the settlement before you sign the papers, otherwise, you could lose everything,' Boban said firmly.

However, Lucy didn't want to discuss it any further. She attempted to steer herself away from the conversation by becoming absorbed in her own thoughts. When Boban repeated his questions, she pretended not to hear him. Then when he tried to speak louder, she quickly put on her AirPods and increased the volume on her phone, signalling that she was not interested in further discussion.

I put a spell on you because you're mine
I can't stand the things that you do
No, no, no, I ain't lying, no
I don't care if you don't want me
'Cause I'm yours, yours, yours, anyhow, yeah
I am yours, yours, yours

This was his favourite song. Adityan's face sparkled in the back of her mind. Her husband and his guitar! This was the same tune that had lured her into believing they were in love when they first kissed on his balcony, next to the Ganges. He was never an easy man to love, or understand, and perhaps that was why she was so drawn to him. She had been just twenty when she fell for her thirty-five-year-old professor. They were friends, then lovers, before taking a vow to stick together through thick and thin.

Years move so fast, like kids who want to grow up. How did I miss that we were changing? How did I not notice that we were growing apart? I blinked, and suddenly everything had changed. Now here I am, alone, with nothing but memories of a love that once was.

7

'The wait is over, Lucy.'

Lucy spent most of the early afternoon sprawled on the luxurious king-size bed of her hotel room. She cried over Adityan and drank from a bottle she had sneaked out of Zacharia's collection. At some point, she slept off, still in her make-up and boots.

When she woke up to the sound of the doorbell in the late evening, she found herself disoriented and lightheaded. Outside, a well-dressed butler in a cute red tie and overcoat inquired if she needed something, to which Lucy screamed, 'Can't you see the 'Do Not Disturb' sign hanging on the knob?'

However, when she caught a glimpse of his sorrowful eyes, her heart softened. The man was only doing his job. It was her current state of mind that rendered every encounter and interaction an unwelcome burden to be managed and navigated.

'Take this—this is the only change I have,' Lucy rummaged through the pockets of her jeans, discovering a tattered hundred-rupee note.

'Madam, we can't accept tips. I merely wanted to inquire if you'd like to order some supper—we have a special Chettinad duck curry and karimeen pollichathu, if you're interested …'

'I don't need anything. Just take this and leave!' She hurled the note towards the young man and slammed the door shut. A moment after her impulsive act, she clenched her jaw. *What am I turning into? Is this who I really am now?*

As she walked back to the bed, the present from Zacharia greeted her from the coffee table in front of the yellow sofa. Standing beside it was a tall, almost translucent figure who asked her: 'Aren't you curious about what's inside?'

'Ahhh!' Lucy jumped back in fear, immediately closing her eyes. *Am I losing it again?* she wondered. First the strange voices, now this. She began massaging her temples in an attempt to calm herself down.

Despite the panic tightening in her chest, an irresistible pull towards the box kept her grounded. Whatever her grandfather had hidden inside, it felt as though it was calling out to her, demanding to be discovered.

After a moment of thought, Lucy grabbed the box and began to unpack it. The outermost layer of the box was made of cardboard, and under it was a thin metal container. Inside that was a gold antique lamp nestled in a bed of bubble wrap. A single-fold handwritten letter rested alongside it.

'What on earth is this? An oil lamp?' Lucy muttered; her annoyance evident as she carefully placed the item on the table.

The lamp appeared ancient but regal. It was draped in a delicate veil of dust, and blue and green gems encircled its handle. She lifted it and studied the inscriptions etched onto its base; the symbols glistened as her gaze roamed over them.

Lucyyyy ... I had been waiting for so long, a whisper reverberated through the room, sending shivers down Lucy's spine. After a moment of hesitation, she reached out to pick up Zacharia's letter.

'My Dear Lucy,

'By the time you read this, my time on this Earth will have drawn to a close, and I will have moved on to the world beyond. When I realised my days were numbered, the first thing that crossed my mind was to whom I should entrust my most precious possession, as it holds powers beyond human comprehension. I am aware that we have not been in touch for quite some time, and both of us share the responsibility for this. Nevertheless, I have faith that you will attend my funeral, and by doing so, this message will reach you at the right moment. Once you comprehend the nature of what I am leaving you, do not let greed overcome you, for that will only invite further destruction.

'Know that your Appappan loves you dearly.'

The brief letter, with Zacharia's elegant long signature at the end, only served to deepen Lucy's confusion and leave her with more questions than answers. She flipped the container over and sifted through every last bit, determined to ensure that there were no bank cheques or legal documents that indicated ownership of anything of value.

As the realisation dawned that she was left with nothing but an old lamp, despair set in. The daunting task of paying off her debts loomed ahead, causing Lucy to feel overwhelmed with anxiety.

When the waves of her anxiety momentarily subsided, she took hold of the lamp and headed to the bathroom to give it a wash. *Maybe it's worth a fortune. Maybe I could auction it off in Bangalore,* she speculated.

Lucy placed the lamp under the faucet and turned the knob all the way. She grabbed her spare toothbrush from a small plastic bag that held her creams and ointments and started scrubbing it clean. As her fingers circled the lamp repeatedly, the whispers that had so far been faint grew louder. 'Let me out … let me out …'

Lucy turned around in panic. *What was that?*

'Harder, dust it harder,' the voice continued. She pressed the brush more firmly, harshly sweeping it around the lamp. 'Once more, once more … more,' the voice urged.

Lucy's fingers moved violently over its surface in a progressing cadence. Then, before she could understand what happened, with an ear-splitting sound, the lamp leapt from her hands and rose into the air. Thick green fumes billowed from it and rapidly filled the room.

Lucy coughed harshly; her eyes watered. 'What the hell!' she screamed, covering her mouth and nose with a bath towel.

The fumes began to swirl, morphing into a dizzying array of complex geometric shapes. Fierce screams, cries and laughs were heard from it. Lucy bolted towards the sofa and leaped onto it, burying her face in the cushions.

'... what in the world is happening?' she yelled, eyes closed. The smoke started spiralling around her, whispering in different voices and lingoes.

When she opened her eyes again, there was a serpent-like creature looming before her, its immense body coiled from end to end. It bore three heads, two of which were superimposed upon the first, with a snub nose and green eyes. The upper head was distinguished by its two cattle horns turned inwards, whereas the other two were of a snake and a man. Lucy felt her legs trembling from fear. Her mouth stayed open and dry. She felt as though she had returned to one of her teenage schizophrenic nightmares.

The creature somehow sensed her fear instantly and began to change shape, transforming from a serpent to an animal, a bird, a reptile, then to a human. 'Are you still afraid?' it inquired in a sly tone.

Lucy remained silent; her head bowed in fear.

The television in her room switched on automatically, channels changed from news, to sports, to Animal Planet, before settling on a movie. The creature approached the device, touching its surface and absorbing its aura. The next moment the creature's form acquired finer details, and its voice transformed to that of the man in the movie. It spoke softly in various languages before settling on the one the movie's actors were speaking in.

'This language is straightforward; its rules are easy to learn,' it remarked, its voice imbued with a tinge of curiosity.

Lucy cast a furtive glance at the creature and took note of its exquisite features—flawless hair, eyelids that hooded beautiful dark eyes flecked with malachite, high cheekbones and an imperious hooked nose. Its wide, simmering mouth was sculpted like that of an Egyptian pharaoh's. But despite its human-like appearance, the creature's right eye burned with an intense green glow while the other eye was lifeless.

Lucy wrapped her arms around her knees and mustered up the courage to speak once more. 'Who … who are you?'

'Who am I?' it bellowed, its laughter booming with such force that Lucy feared the ceiling would crumble upon her. 'I am magic, the resident of the lamp. Named God, devil, djinn, I reign. Kingdoms rise and fall by my hand, but for thee I am a slave—a humble servant seeking a master.'

A djinn? What the fuc …? Lucy's eyebrows shot up, her mind a whirlwind of confusion as she scrambled to process the bizarre turn of events. *When did I last take my medication? Am I having another episode? Why now?*

Her thoughts meandered into the past, to those days confined in a room at Palathikal House. Although the specifics of that time eluded her, she remembered encountering the unreal—things that defied explanation. *It might be the stress,* she brooded, recalling articles from monthly health magazines that spoke of post-traumatic stress disorder sufferers grappling with hallucinations.

'You humans, always so delicate, like fine china on the verge of breaking. You are all forever trying to reason away the reality staring you in the face,' the djinn teased. 'I'm no hallucination. You've known about me, haven't you? It's right there in your memories …'

The television screen began to quiver, monochromatic pixels gradually consuming the display. To her surprise, Lucy saw her younger self sitting in her grandparents' room, attentively watching an old Onida television. Upon closer inspection, she realised that her past self was engrossed in a documentary called *Debunking Fairy Tales.*

'Throughout human history, creatures with supernatural abilities and mysterious origins have captivated the human imagination. Legends of beings like djinns, falaks and ghouls have persisted for centuries, passed down through generations of stories, myths and folklore. Despite their cultural differences, these creatures share a common thread of otherworldliness and are often depicted as possessing magical powers beyond human understanding. Can they be real?' an impeccably dressed professor confidently shared his research findings before an audience in the United States.

'No, no, no, no … Not possible!' Lucy screamed out. With a sudden burst of energy, she leaped from the sofa and raced towards the bathroom, frantically stripping off her clothes before jumping under the showerhead and twisting the knob to full blast. The ice-cold water sent shivers down her spine as she gasped for air, her mouth opening wide to take in as much oxygen as possible.

As she stood there, drenched and trembling, she repeated to herself over and over again, 'This is all in my head. It's all just in my head.'

'What should I call you, master? Do you have a name?' inquired the djinn, suddenly appearing beside her. 'If my appearance frightens you, I'll shift form to something small and new, perhaps a pup, a feline or feathered friend, whatever aligns with your world view.'

'Stop talking to me … Stop … You are just in my head … Just in my head, a speck of my imagination. I shouldn't have missed my medication,' shouted Lucy with shivering lips, before hastily pulling the translucent shower curtain around her. 'Lucy, this is just a dream. You are asleep. You'll wake up soon … just stay calm,' she reassured herself.

'O master, hear my whispered plea, this is no fantasy. Any dream of yours could come true. All you must do is make a wish.' Hovering above her, the djinn darted like an insect dancing near a flame. 'I could tell you who I am, my name even, if it helps to ease your nerves.'

'You have a name?' Lucy murmured, asking herself why she was continuing to engage with him.

'All djinns have names. They are leashes that keep us bound to magic. All those who know our name have power over us.'

'There are others like you? What are you?' Lucy asked in desperation, still wondering when her body would decide to wake up.

'I am Iblis, lord of all the demons and djinns, made from the fires beneath the seventh earth. I was once an angel, who flew with Jibrael, Mikael, Israfil and Azrael, but not anymore.' The djinn started laughing wildly. 'But fear me not, since I am nothing but a slave to the magic that brought me to this world. Your wish is my command, master. It is only through you that I can be free.'

'Don't call me master. I have a name, Lucy,' she grunted.

'Oh, Lucy, a child of light,' he sang with a smirk. 'If granted a wish, what would you choose? Wealth beyond measure that you would never lose? To possess all your eyes can see? Is that not what you humans desire?'

Lucy remained silent, but her mind couldn't help but ponder upon it.

Does he always sing? Is that how he talks? she thought. *What if he is who he claims to be? What if I have wishes like Aladdin?*

After lingering in silence for several fleeting moments, she turned off the shower, drew the curtain aside and walked straight back to the room. The djinn accompanied her like a floating bubble, gently wringing out her wet hair with a white towel. 'Humans are fragile, Lucy. Let me keep your hair dry,' he whispered.

8

'Rules of the djinns are simple,' said Iblis. He hovered over Lucy, who sat on the sofa in clean clothes and her hair wrapped in a towel. 'You have three wishes, three desires, that your heart seeks. You cannot wish for endless wishes or eternal life, for it is your nature to be mortal and mine to be immortal. You may not wish for the dead; they do not want to be disturbed and I cannot absolve sin or end all suffering. And then there is love, what no sorcery could tame.'

'I have no wishes,' Lucy repeated, keeping her arms crossed.

'No wishes? Humans always have something they want, even if they don't realise it yet,' said Iblis with a chuckle. 'Why not wish for power? Wealth? Beautiful men who would dance and feed you grapes?'

Out of nowhere, two strikingly handsome men draped in luxurious silk robes materialised. In their hands was a shimmering golden bowl filled to the brim with luscious Arabian grapes. They playfully placed a few grapes on her lips, but Lucy immediately spat them out.

'Leave me alone,' she shouted. Her hands frantically flailed around, shooing the men away.

'Aha, I see now. You don't seem to fancy men, do you?' Iblis quipped, his hand swirling through the air in a mesmerising motion. Suddenly, the two men before Lucy transformed—their faces contorted, their chests broadened and their hips widened as they danced around her with effortless grace, singing in a language Lucy had never heard before.

'Please, I need some space. I need to take things slow,' she begged.

'I have all the time in the world, Lucy. Time is not my concern.' Iblis nodded at the dancers, and they soon disappeared. 'But this is about my freedom. I have been waiting for a master for a very, very long time. I don't want to be a slave for another thousand years, waiting for someone to pick me up. Why not make a wish?'

'I have no wishes, Iblis,' Lucy groaned, laying back on the sofa.

'Use your imagination, Lucy, that is all you need.' Iblis transformed his appearance. He now looked like a psychiatrist, complete with a white chair to sit on and a notepad in his hands. 'Why not talk about your problems? Maybe we can solve them first?'

'Hold on a minute.' Lucy raised her head and examined the djinn's outfit. 'How do you even know what a psychiatrist looks like? You're supposed to be new to this world.'

'Ah, I see why you're confused. Although it may seem like I am new to this world, the truth is that I have watched it since its very beginning.' Iblis took a deep breath, causing the entire room to vibrate.

'As a djinn, no era is ever completely new to us.' He took a book from the table. With a wave of his hand, the words from the book lifted off the pages and flowed into his body. 'You see, we are beings of pure energy, and everything in this world is made up of it as well. We can learn and adapt to any era in just a few moments.'

'Beings of pure energy? What does that even mean?'

'Allow me to demonstrate.' The djinn swirled his hands. 'Calm your mind, pay attention and observe me closely.'

Lucy could suddenly see intricate layers of pulsating energy, each one in a different hue and pattern, flowing into the djinn. Lucy rubbed her eyes in disbelief, trying to make sense of what she was observing.

'There is much in this world that humans are not supposed to see.' Iblis leaned closer to Lucy, his voice low and serious. He moved his fingers, and suddenly one of the energy waves became thin and thread-like. With a focused grip, he pulled on it, causing it to widen. 'And this is what you humans call radio waves.' Suddenly, Lucy could hear faint, crackling static noises emanating from the air.

What in the world is happening here? Her mouth fell wide open.

'Leave that for now,' Iblis said, his voice reassuring. 'You'll eventually get the hang of it. That's what happens when you're close to me. Secrets of the universe present themselves.' He polished his psychiatrist glasses, carefully placed them back on his nose and leaned back in his chair. 'Now, Lucy darling, let's get back to your problems.'

'I don't have any,' Lucy said. Her voice sounded unconvincing even to herself. Adityan's face suddenly popped up in front of her. 'I am your biggest problem,' he said confidently. 'No, you are not. You still love me,' she muttered under her breath, trying to push away the emotions that were threatening to overwhelm her.

Lucy's eyes drifted off as a deluge of memories washed over her.

Now, she could almost feel the warmth of Adityan's body next to hers, how peaceful he looked when he slept, and how she would lay there for hours, watching him breathe. She recalled the sensation of his stubble brushing against her skin during tender kisses, and the way his cologne seemed to linger in the air long after he had left the room. *He must be in the office, taking care of important matters. He must be keeping himself busy to forget me.*

Lucy couldn't help but feel a sense of longing and sadness wash over her as she realised just how much she missed him.

Last year at this time, they were busy decorating their cozy new apartment in Koramangala. They would spend hours making lists of all the things they needed: a wide ninety-eight–inch television, a top-of-the-line washing machine, a sleek refrigerator and Ikea furniture they would build together. They argued over which sofa to choose, and its colour and size.

On some days, their arguments escalated into physical confrontations. He would overpower her with his strength and hold her tightly under his arms, leaving bruises and scars. They would break things and decide to go their separate ways. *But isn't that what everyone calls love? Always keeping the other on the edge? Adityan still loves me. He will come back.*

'So, there is a man?' Iblis tapped the pen twice on the notepad, waking Lucy from her train of thoughts.

'A man?'

'I know you more than you realise, Lucy, and being so close to you now, I can feel your emotions and sense your thoughts before they even pop into your mind.'

'Do you even know what feelings mean?'

'Djinns are no exception to the charms of love. We are bound to its magic like we are to the lamp. And in my humble opinion, it is the strongest thing in the cosmos, one that transcends space and time,' Iblis replied. He spread his palms wide, revealing within them miniature versions of the sun, the planets and the stars. 'Does love's essence reside solely within humanity's embrace, or does it grace all beings with its ineffable grace?'

'What?'

'You see, Lucy, love's unyielding force binds all things as one—the planet to the sun, the moon to Earth and stars to the beyond. But man calls it gravitation, reducing nature to his limited perception, forgetting that each of them is a soul in motion, dancing to the rhythm of the cosmos.' The djinn let out a laugh. 'You humans are a curious kind, thinking that you've come so far. Yet you move in circles, striving to define the infinite. You forget that you're a mirror of the universe's soul, a reflection of its every facet. Your love is love itself, the same that flows through the living and the dead, and we are all but a fleeting spark in its boundless expanse.'

'Do you always sing and complicate things?' Lucy asked, in awe of the djinn's profound insight.

'My voice echoes the ineffable, for poetry alone can convey its essence. But its true beauty lies in how you listen to it, in the way the heart opens up to its notes and allows the poetry to bloom.'

'Is poetry all that you are into?'

'No. I tell stories, tales from the past. Would you like to hear one?'

'Can you tell me the story of how you got trapped in this lamp?'

'Ah, look at you, Lucy, the child of light, full of magic yourself, reading a djinn's mind. It was my first incarceration.'

'First?'

'I may be a djinn made of magical dust, but I'm also a fool who fell in love with a mortal. I should have been more cautious, but no one warned me, not even my divine masters,' Iblis whispered in her ears. His voice was so low that Lucy mistook it for her own thoughts.

'How were you caught in the first place?' she asked.

'By desire. How else?'

9

'After the death of Pharaoh Thutmose II, his sister Hatshepsut used her political cunning and religious power to reign over Egypt. It was fate that brought the young queen to power because destiny makes no mistakes,' the djinn began his tale.

The television in front of Lucy crackled and clicked, and images of fifteenth-century Egypt began to play on the screen. The display gradually expanded, filling her entire field of vision, transporting her into another world.

'As expected, one of the first things Hatshepsut did after ascending the throne was to hail the best sorcerers from across Persia to learn about the lost art of black magic. Her father, the great king Thutmose, always prayed to powers beyond him and favoured sacrifices to the old gods, so it was no accident his daughter inherited his natural inclination to indulge in the occult powers. As part of an elaborate plan, Hatshepsut prepared herself to summon magical creatures from the worlds above that were invisible to humans.

'From the moment of her birth, Hatshepsut had been looked down upon by the royal family for being born a woman. This burden had shaped her character, moulding her into a person thirsty for power. Now, with the throne within her grasp, she sought divine help to claim absolute control over the vast Egyptian empire.

'The sorcerers who aided her demanded human and animal sacrifices to call out to the underworld and the heavens for attention. They told her the way forward was through blood and gore. Many firstborn human children and animals were brought from the streets and their throats slit; their life forces were used to call out to the ancient beings of unimaginable power.

'When Iblis, the king of djinns, heard her call, it came as a song—a lullaby that summoned him to Earth. It lured the magical being from the upper realms of the sky to the Deir el-Bahri in Egypt, to the pharaoh's palace. He witnessed the beautiful Hatshepsut, who sat inside a heptagram drawn in blood and bones. In her hands, she held a harp and played tunes that could mesmerise even the gods. The djinn was soon in love with her.

'Every night from then on, the djinn watched Hatshepsut from the shadows and whispered to her through dreams. He counselled her on how to rule Egypt and warned her about the dangers that lay in the future. Her enemies were annihilated, and everything naturally fell under her reign. Politicians, aristocrats and powerful merchants eventually bowed down to her rule, and wealth started pouring in from all parts of the world.

'As Hatshepsut's enchantment grew stronger, other magical creatures like efrits, qareens and falaks started appearing in front of her palace—all hopelessly in love with the queen. But Iblis stood in the gates and threatened them to never return. He screeched, "This human belongs to me, return to where you're from."

'However, as the queen continued to master the old dark spells, her powers grew stronger and more potent. She began to summon more powerful and ominous entities from the outer worlds. Iblis grew desperate. One day, he took on the shape of a sailor from the land of Punt and arrived at Hatshepsut's court, bearing gifts of ebony and gold atop a hundred elephants. But Hatshepsut, with her newly honed mystical senses, immediately saw through Iblis's disguise. She knew that it was he who had been whispering to her at night; he was the true source of her prosperity. She embraced him without hesitation and asked him to accompany her to the seclusion of her royal chamber.

'That was the start of a passionate love affair between the djinn and the queen.

'During their time together, Iblis was not a slave to the lamp. He was a supreme magical being who helped his pharaoh gather great wealth and control. He called her Maatkare out of love and granted every wish she expressed.

'Even though Hatshepsut was aware of his name, she never divulged it to anyone—she knew the power it held.

'Like two wanderers on an endless quest to discover the unknown, they ventured far and wide, constantly seeking out new adventures. They hunted in Hercynian Forest, saw Aztec temples in Tenochtitlan and rode wild horses in Mali. Along the way, they discussed philosophy, religion and politics. Iblis taught her about the stars and planets, explaining the intricacies of the universe in a way that only a djinn could.

'With every passing moment, their connection deepened, and Hatshepsut's ability to communicate with the supernatural grew stronger. Soon, she found herself enveloped in a world of magic, where she could read the djinn's thoughts and vividly experience his memories through visions and dreams.

'To a mere mortal, it was a euphoric sensation, a potent elixir more powerful than any known substance. Entranced, she journeyed alongside him to realms beyond the known, from the celestial heavens to the fiery depths of hell, witnessing through his eyes the vastness of his past life.

'As the years trickled by, immersed in the boundless love that they shared, she lost track of time. But as it does for all, time eventually called for them to return to reality. Hatshepsut resumed her position as the pharaoh, her thirst for the djinn sated, and she started wondering what lay beyond him.

'Having triumphed over neighbouring territories and filled her chambers with myrrh and the green gold of Emu, the queen decided to come up with a new request. She asked Iblis to help her build a temple that would stand the test of time, a massive structure opposite the city of Luxor.

'"Iblis," said the queen with a determined look in her eyes, "I want you to construct something so breathtakingly beautiful that even the gods themselves would be consumed with envy. It must be a symbol of my power and authority, one that will leave no doubt in the minds of mortals that I am the rightful ruler of this land."

'"Your wish is my command," Iblis bowed down.

'Every night after the sun went down, he summoned his mystical powers to craft three towering terraces that rose high above the barren desert floor. In time, an awe-inspiring marvel emerged from the cliffs of Deir el-Bahari, a sight that left all who beheld it speechless with wonder. Its ethereal glow lit up the surrounding desert, drawing visitors from far and wide to gaze upon its splendour.

'But things were about to take a drastic turn, as the queen's heart began to wander towards a new love—Senenmut, the master architect of the temple. With his olive skin, curly locks and youthful looks, he bewitched her with his allure.

'Aware of the djinn's burning love for her, Hatshepsut ordered him to stand guard outside her chambers, warning him that any attempt to interfere with her trysts would be met with severe consequences. Iblis, hopelessly devoted to the queen, could do nothing but obey her orders.

'He knew that if he failed her, Hatshepsut would cast him away, replacing him with a more obedient servant. With a heavy heart, he stood outside her chambers, listening to the sounds of his beloved Hatshepsut and her new lover.'

'Love is not always as it appears, Lucy,' Iblis murmured in her ears as she watched the rest of his story unfold. 'It can be deceitful and manipulative, ensnaring you in its enchantments and making you its slave. And though my queen kept me by her side, Senenmut was a nefarious man with dishonourable ambitions. He wanted me to leave, so he convinced my queen to divulge my true name. Love can be fickle and dangerous, you see, so it is important to be wary of those who seek to use it for their gain.'

The source of a djinn's power lies solely in their name; it was that name the almighty uttered thrice when the djinns were first brought from the magic dust that rests in the fires of hell. Their names brought them under someone's control or released them from any binding spell.

When Iblis revealed his name to Hatshepsut, his intention was for her to access some of his power. He was aware that when mortals acquire his name in his presence, they also become a conduit for supernatural energy and can develop their own magical abilities. Consequently, the queen gained the ability to speak, read and understand any language and communicate with people in their native tongue. As she made the critical mistake of revealing Iblis's name to a near stranger, she set in motion a chain of events that carried vast repercussions for both the djinn and the queen.

Senenmut, aided by his sorcerers, cast a strong spell on Iblis, trapping him within a lamp. And as his body began to vanish, Iblis used the last of his magical strength to caution his queen. 'Oh, wise Hatshepsut, do not let his love fool you,' he cried out. 'Senenmut's heart yearns for something cruel and insidious. He will be the one to take your life in an insatiable quench for power. Be cautious, my queen, for he is not to be trusted.'

Despite Iblis's words of caution, Hatshepsut remained enthralled by her new love and turned a deaf ear to the warning.

Once the djinn was trapped inside the lamp, Senenmut ordered his most loyal soldiers to set sail across the Red Sea and hurl it into the ocean. The lamp was thrown away, never to be found again.

For the first hundred years of his captivity, Iblis raged against his fate. He prayed to Zephyrkolo for release, and when that didn't work he begged any and all gods he knew or could think of for help. 'O, Divine Lords, hear my humble plea. Release me from these confines, and I shall be a faithful servant to thee. With powers over mortal men, I shall ensure your names will stay alive in the annals of history; they shall remain glorious, divine and without stain,' he sang to them in desperation.

When his prayers went unanswered, he retreated into his waking dreams, replaying every moment of his life over and over again.

To keep his sanity, Iblis created his own reality within the cramped space of the lamp, trying to mirror his lost kingdom in the heavens. He crafted a throne, a sceptre, a maze and a luminous sphere through which he could observe the human world.

From the tiny aperture of the lamp, he kept a watchful eye on people and attempted to signal for their assistance. 'Beneath the briny depths lies the King of Djinns, whose power and might exceed all whims, seek him out with courage and skill, and your heart's desires he shall fulfil,' he sang in people's dreams. But no one came to his rescue. Eventually, everything became tiresome for the djinn. So he returned to his rage and his prayers, into a deep meditation.

In due course, as predicted, Hatshepsut's life came to a tragic end. Once her trusted djinn was sent away, Senenmut poisoned her to death.

10

'Greed—the suffocating stench of it.'

It was the knock on the door that woke Lucy the next day.

She was sprawled on the sofa, hair cocooned in a towel and her naked body partially exposed. As the morning sun streamed through the windows, she pondered the reality of last night's occurrences. It wasn't uncommon for her to experience unanticipated episodes of psychosis. Anxiously, she wondered if the hallucination would endure.

When the subtle knocks on the door did not get a response, the visitor pressed the calling bell, a melodious tone that resembled a cuckoo bird.

Oh, these door boys! Forever oblivious. Why can't they simply pay attention? Lucy fixed her clothes and sprang to the door.

Outside stood Boban the lawyer dressed in freshly laundered clothes and sporting his usual grin. 'Must have been a busy night, right, Lucy molae?' he remarked, stepping into the room without asking for permission.

'I just woke up,' Lucy replied grumpily, disapproving of her uninvited guest. *What does this clown want?*

'I was wondering about our conversation in the car yesterday, about your divorce and if you needed representation,' Boban said as he made himself comfortable on the couch and placed his bag on the table. 'After all, ya are my Zacharia sir's granddaughter, and it is my duty to make sure you are taken care of in times of need.'

These humans, always lying, always so greedy for more, someone said in her ears. Shocked, Lucy looked around to see who was around.

'By the way, did you happen to open that box? Was it the old lamp?' Boban asked, leaning in attentively. 'I didn't see it on the list of items Zacharia sir left behind in his collection.'

'Do you know anything about it? Where did Appapan get it from?'

'Aaa, so it is that,' Boban said, grinning broadly. 'Zacharia sir never really spoke about it much, but we brought some experts from England fifteen–twenty years ago to check it out. They told him that the lamp is a rare artefact from Egypt, way back from 15 AD. And if I remember correctly, one of them fellas, Howard Evans or Howard Fleming or somethin' like that, was a professor from Cambridge. He asked Zacharia sir to sell it to him!'

'And?'

'Aye, and nothing. Zacharia sir told him point-blank, "It's not for sale." That fellow was ready to throw over a quarter of a million British pounds at him, a damn fortune, but Zacharia sir wouldn't budge,' Boban complained 'But molae, if you're lookin' to sell it, I know some well-connected people in Mumbai who can help you out. I'll make some calls and they'll set up an auction for ya in no time, no problem at all.'

I warned you. The old rascal is just as greedy as his father and grandfather, and the one before him. They all met a miserable end, filled with pain and regret, the whispers continued.

'So, your aunt Gracy told me you're havin' some trouble with loans and the bank's sent ya an eviction notice. Is that right?' the man asked, slowly getting to the point of his visit. 'What's the amount ya need to pay 'em?'

'It is a lot, Boban uncle,' Lucy said, covering her face with her palm. The headache and angst returned. She started scratching her knees. She wanted to scream that the debts were not her cross to bear but a shared responsibility. Still, the words never came; she feared that voicing her grievances would only emphasise her own sense of failure, so she opted for a mask of helplessness.

As her apprehension reached a breaking point and her body seemed to seize up, Lucy's gaze was drawn to the nearly empty bottle on the floor, its last vestiges clinging tenaciously to the bottom. *Should I call room service for a bottle of rum? What if I max out my credit limit? Would Adityan be notified?*

One thought leading to another, she soon found herself immersed in a memory of when she and Adityan were living together in a small two-room apartment overlooking the Ganges. One day, they were tipsy on Bombay Sapphire and relishing some aloo kachori they had purchased on their way back from the office.

'What should we name it?' she had asked, constantly munching on the street food.

'Picasso,' he replied. 'Find the Next Picasso and Bring Home a Masterpiece—that would be our tagline.'

'We will make this a big thing, won't we? Together?' she asked, unable to contain her happiness.

'It would be like Murthy and Infosys, Ambani and Reliance, Jobs and Apple,' he had joked. 'We'll be so big that every investor in the country will line up for an appointment with us.'

'We will be called visionaries who saved struggling artists from their capitalistic bosses and corporate jobs.'

Together, they burst into boisterous laughter, marvelling at the audacity of their aspirations. That moment marked the beginning of their ambitious venture, the one that eventually spiralled out of her control.

Six months from that day, they had exhausted not only their savings but also the money they had borrowed from banks. Fearing a looming failure of their start-up, Adiyan had urged Lucy to call her grandfather and request a feature in his *Daily Malayalam* newspaper. However, Lucy rejected the suggestion by giving the same reason every time. 'I don't want my family involved in this mess. I don't need their help. This is our project, and we will fix it ourselves.'

But eventually she, too, realised that the company was going under when two of their early engineers left after they were unable to pay their salaries.

'Appappa, I need some help,' she had called Zacharia that evening.

'When are you coming home, Lucy? Your grandmother keeps asking about you. She is sick, worse than before,' the old man replied in a grumpy voice.

'We started a company here, and I was hoping you could help us with some publicity. Can you ask one of your editors to interview us?' Lucy had requested, still feeling a little uneasy about her request.

'We?'

'It is me and Adityan; we started this together.'

'Who's Adityan?'

'He is someone I like,' she replied.

There was a long silence at the other end, before the phone got disconnected.

Three weeks after that call, Adityan and Lucy were featured on a YouTube channel run by an upcoming social media influencer who went by the name 'IndianBusinessFuture'. And to everyone's surprise, the interview went viral, garnering four million views in less than two months. In no time, media agencies across the country started bombarding them with interview requests and their faces were everywhere.

Picasso became the most downloaded app on Play Store, bringing over a million new users on board.

While Adityan was the public face of their business, Lucy became the driving force behind the product. She tirelessly worked on improving the service and built strategic partnerships with art galleries, auction houses and collectors. Through their hard work and dedication, the app quickly expanded across borders, becoming one of the fastest-growing digital businesses from India.

However, this growth came at a cost.

As the person in charge of finances in the early days, Lucy had to take out significant personal loans to ensure Picasso's survival. And later, even with larger investors coming in, she never paid the loans back.

'Give me a number, any number. How much we talkin' here?' Boban's question brought her back to the present.

'Around three crore rupees. And then there's the interest. I took it for the business's operating costs.'

'Oh, oh oh oh,' the lawyer made a strange noise with a faint smile. 'That's a lotta money.' Without saying another word, the man reached into his bag and produced bundles of thousand-rupee notes, which he carefully spread out on the dark wooden table in front of him.

Once he had Lucy's undivided attention, he spoke again. 'This is around forty-five lakh. It's a small advance, if the sale goes through. It is a risk for me though. Maybe ya can call up your bank and use this to extend the eviction for a few more weeks.'

Don't listen to him, Lucy, Iblis's voice sounded in her ear. *His heart is in the wrong place. He will only lead you to disappointment.*

'Don't think too much about it, this is a good deal. And my commission's just 10 per cent of the sale,' he said, packing up the bundles into his duffle bag before placing it by her feet. After thinking for a few minutes, Lucy reached out and pulled the bag closer. Boban's face lit up like he'd just won the lottery. He patted her shoulder and made his way out.

He turned around at the door and said, 'I'll come back tomorrow with some legal papers. You might have to sign over your power of attorney to me before the sale.'

11

'I've had enough of dealing with fools, I'm going nowhere.' Iblis materialised out of thin air as soon as Boban left the room. His face was etched with boredom, which somehow made him appear angrier. 'You humans are perplexing creatures. Why be satisfied with a mere bag of dirt when the whole world is within reach? Make a wish, and everything you desire shall be yours.'

'All that I desire will just come to me?' Lucy chuckled sarcastically, feeling both mesmerised and shocked by the extent of her loose mind.

Iblis stared at her, disappointed.

'I have nothing for you, Mr Djinn. No wish, no demand. I am nothing. I am empty. I am lost,' she murmured in a low, broken voice.

'Not what a djinn offering wishes wants to hear,' Iblis complained. 'You are a wise and cautious woman, Lucy. I know why you hesitate to trust me. But we all have desires, even if we don't always know what they are.'

Iblis looked at the duffel bag brimming with fresh notes. His fingers moved in a peculiar fashion and the cash inside it stared doubling. First, the bag expanded, then ballooned, finally bursting open, and money poured out of it to the floor. But it did not stop there. Thousand-rupee notes kept appearing out of nothingness and covered the marble floor.

Lucy's eyebrows went up and she scratched her head hard. *Is this real or all in my head?* She closed her eyes and tried to imagine something else—something pleasant, ordinary, less stressful.

The first thought that came to her mind was of her childhood pet, Tipu. It put a smile on her face. Lucy focused on the happy feeling. She saw his cute, chubby face with its big, expressive brown eyes staring back at her. Then his floppy ears and the constantly wagging tail. Out of nowhere, a wave of sadness washed over Lucy as she realised that she hadn't gone to see Tipu even once after leaving home. *Why have I been so cold-hearted? I wish I could rewind time and make things right.* Tears welled up in her eyes, and with that the fears she had been evading broke free.

Despite trying to push them away, the faces of her parents crept into her mind. They asked if she was okay. She angrily shouted at them to leave her alone, to let her be at peace. They were never there for her when she needed them, so why should she care now? If there was one thing she could wish for, it would be to relive her childhood, she thought. But then she remembered the overwhelming grief and betrayal she felt when they died, and she couldn't bear to go through that again. *Why would anyone want to endure all that pain?*

Lucy started laughing at herself for letting this ridiculous fairy tale get to her.

Zacharia, her beloved grandfather, should have known not to mess with her already fragile mind. It was true that they hadn't spoken since she got married without asking for his permission.

But she was in love, and she hadn't meant to hurt anyone. *Love just happens sometimes, and there's nothing one can do about it.*

She wondered if, in his final moments, Zacharia had been able to forgive her. But it seemed that was not the case.

Look at that lamp. It was a clear sign that he didn't care enough to leave her anything worthwhile. Now she had to navigate through crowded auction houses and pay back her debts. And who knows, maybe someone would see how weak she was and take advantage of it. They would cast her aside and take everything that she owned—just like Jancy chechi.

The fear of losing everything was too much to bear and Lucy couldn't keep her hands still. Her thoughts were out of control. She scratched her head wildly, her nails digging into her scalp. She tried to be as rough as possible, so the pain would distract her from her good-for-nothing life.

How could he? How could he push me way like I don't matter? Lucy thought as she clenched her teeth.

Out of everyone who had turned against her, Adityan's betrayal hurt the most. *Our time together, was it even real? Or did I imagine it all?*

The pain felt unbearable, she couldn't hold back the tears that streamed down her face. *I need a drink, today is the day I would drink myself to death.* She stood up in search of a room phone.

'Hello, room service?'

'Yes, madam.'

'Can you bring a bottle of rum to my room?'

'Yes, certainly, madam. Which brand would you like to have?'

'Do you have Bacardi Carta Blanka?'

'We don't, madam.'

'Then send someone to get it, I can pay extra.' She looked at the money scattered on the floor.

'Okay, madam. It will be delivered shortly.'

Lucy disconnected the call.

You should have asked me, the djinn laughed from the side. 'Shuttttt upppp! I need some peace of mind,' she screamed. And before those screams ended, she began to see unfamiliar faces in her mind's eye.

A lanky, youthful figure stood patiently on the bustling sidewalk with other pedestrians. He wore a vibrant red tie and sleek black overcoat, just like the hotel employee who came knocking on her last evening. Across from him was a bar with a dazzling array of posters featuring rugged, bearded models, all flaunting a particular brand of whiskey.

The young man slipped into a shadowy alleyway, nimbly navigating his way to the bar's counter. He presented the bartender with a scrap of paper, and in exchange received a frosty bottle of Bacardi Carta Blanka.

On his way back, he took the longer path to the back door of the hotel. While walking, he carefully peeled the sticker around the bottle's neck and opened it. After making sure no one was watching him, he quickly took a swig of the liquid inside. Then, with the same care he had shown in removing it, he replaced the sticker and screwed the cap back tightly.

'You feel that, Lucy? You see that?' the djinn's voice came like a harpoon to her thoughts, pulling her away from the visions.

'What is this?'

'Encountering an immortal djinn unveils new powers held within. Mortal flesh becomes the conduit for supernatural energies to take root,' the djinn hummed. 'Fear not, for no burden greater than you can handle would be given. The powers bestowed are a key to unlock your true destiny. Liberation is not mine alone, but yours too.'

'That's a load of bullshit, you are full of …'

'Your mind is clouded with the man who broke your heart. He is the chain you need to break first.' Ilbis perched on the sofa and crossed his legs. He waved his hands over her head, soaking up the emotional waves emanating from her thoughts.

'A man? My mind is clouded by a man?'

'In the world of djinn, everything is energy. We are the masters of all physical and mental matter,' he said.

Lucy nodded.

'I can sense your thoughts, the waves of pain stemming from your heart. They are true and profound, flowing from the core of your being. I see someone you loved and then tried to forget. It is his memories that stand out from the rest.' Iblis opened his palm to reveal a small three-dimensional figure of a man. He sat on a pale couch, checking his phone and constantly staring at the door of his apartment. 'This is your Hatshepsut, the one who will teach you about love and its suffering.'

Lucy's eyes narrowed as she scrutinised the tiny figure, recognising the familiar features of her husband's face.

'Make a wish,' Iblis uttered.

'Take me where he is, show me what he has been doing since we separated,' Lucy commanded. The djinn's lips curved into a wide smile as his body began to expand like a balloon filled with air. His body shimmered and transformed, illuminating the room with its otherworldly glow. His huge smile blinded her. 'Your wish is my command,' a thunderous voice boomed.

12

Even though they were watching the man from above, Lucy could see everything about him in detail—what he wore, where he sat and what played on the television screen in front of him. She could even see the messages his phone received and how microorganisms changed on reading them. It was as if time and space were under her command. Like a scientist watching microorganisms under the microscope, she focused on and off at Adityan and the things around him.

'Is this how the gods watch us from above?' she asked in surprise.

'Which gods?' the djinn laughed. 'Gods are not interested in the acts of humans, they have their own lives to figure out. In the grand scheme of things, no life is more important than another. All of us are playing our part.'

'Is this now?'

'What is now but a passing moment, a fleeting intersection of the past and the future.'

'You know what I mean.'

'For in your quest to define "the now", you must confront the fluidity of time itself, the paradox of your existence—that you are both anchored in the present moment and yet forever slipping away from it, caught in an endless cycle of becoming and passing away. So perhaps the question is not "Is this now?" but rather, "What does it mean to be present in a world that is always in motion?"'

'Okay, enough, thank you for complicating things further.'

'My pleasure.'

As their conversation continued, Adityan's doorbell rang twice, and he ran towards it in a hurry. Standing outside was a young woman dressed elegantly in a loose blue sari. He welcomed her inside and asked her to sit comfortably on the couch in the living room. While she perused his impeccably organised home, taking note of the various certificates and accolades displayed on the walls, Adityan slipped into the kitchen and emerged with a bottle of Jack Daniel's, a pair of glasses and a platter of cashews.

'Shruthy, how do you like my modest home?'

'It is beautiful, sir, but I was under the impression that we were going out for dinner,' she said, eyeing the alcohol that was coming her way.

'Oh, we're just warming up. We'll be heading out soon.' He sat opposite her and opened the bottle. 'By the way, you look beautiful in that sari. It suits you.'

'Sir, I was a little confused when you asked me out on a date because I thought you were married.'

'Drop the "sir", Adityan is fine,' he said, smiling wildly. The girl's face brightened up. 'And by the way, I'm not married. Who told you that? I'm single and ready to mingle.'

'I heard some talk in the office that you're married and getting divorced, and that the earlier CFO was your wife,' she said, sounding unsure. 'But I know people trash-talk successful people like you all the time.'

'Take the glass, Shruthy. Forget those backstabbing bastards. Let them be,' he said, taking his half-filled glass of whiskey on the rocks and raising it in the air. 'Let's make this a memorable night, and cheers to all the success that awaits us in the future.'

Lucy couldn't bear to watch anymore and averted her gaze from the room. Her eyes teared up and the sights before her became blurred. She turned her head towards Iblis and spoke softly. 'Grief is an odd thing, isn't it? People respond to it differently. Maybe this is how Adityan is coping with it, don't you think?'

'Is that what you truly believe, Lucy? Or are you deceiving yourself?' the djinn replied, his tone cold and distant. 'To see things clearly, accept them as they appear. Illusions will only mislead you, do not seek comfort from them.'

'Adityan is a good man, he cares for me. We had our differences, but our love was real,' she groaned.

Iblis smiled mischievously at her stern face.

The djinn snapped his fingers, and a flash of lightning lit up the sky. Suddenly, as if Lucy had tuned into a radio, a male voice began to play in the background—Adityan's. The view in front of her cleared up, and she could see his apartment again. But this time she could hear Adityan's and Shruthy's thoughts too.

Oh, look at that, look at that, I should have called her earlier. Adityan's eyes traced the exquisite lines of Shruthy's shapely legs, her exposed waist and the bulge in her blouse. In the sultry cadence of his voice Lucy detected an unmistakable scent of lust, a potent sensation that enveloped him in its powerful grasp.

He poured more alcohol into the girl's glass before moving closer. 'So, Shruthy, we're looking for a marketing head for our new franchise in Mumbai.' His hands slowly made their way to her lap. 'Would you be interested? It pays five times more than your current event management position.'

The fervour of desire escalated, surpassing the intoxicating grasp of the alcohol they were consuming. Images of her nude body and the way it would sway beneath him looped persistently in his thoughts.

'Ahhh ... I'm definitely interested, but am I qualified?' The young girl giggled as the alcohol lowered her inhibitions. *What does he really want? Did he plan all this?* her mind started chattering.

Lucy's eyes widened and she felt like puking. She turned to the djinn to halt this game he was playing with her, but Iblis didn't care.

'There are always ways to climb the corporate ladder, but everything comes at a price.' Adityan took his phone and connected it to the music system. He opened a playlist called 'Romantic evenings' and pressed on a song.

I put a spell on you because you're mine
I can't stand the things that you do
No, no, no, I ain't lying, no
I don't care if you don't want me
Cause I'm yours, yours, yours, anyhow, yeah
I am yours, yours, yours

'Stop, stop ... Iblis, enough, enough ... I understand what you are trying to tell me,' Lucy cried out, her anxiety surging. She pointed a threatening finger at the djinn, her eyes filled with menace. However, Iblis stood unshaken, his eyes steady and unflinching as they met hers.

'Lucy, my dear, know that pain is a portal through which growth and immortal wisdom arrives. Life is more than a few fleeting moments, it's an evolution of the mind that your soul seeks.' The djinn now hummed in a high pitch. 'Pain, problems and strife you cannot flee, for they are the means to set you free, embrace them with open arms, and discover new beginnings without end.'

'Stop vomiting that goddamn poetry and get me out of here! I've learnt my damn lesson and I'm sick of this crap!'

Iblis snapped his finger again. Immediately, the voices toned down and images before her faded. The next instant, they were back in the hotel room, on the sofa where they sat before.

'How did you enjoy your first wish, Lucy? Was love as beautiful as you thought?' Iblis mocked.

'First wish? What do you mean?' Lucy replied, feigning ignorance. 'I don't recall making any wishes.'

'You asked me to show him.' Iblis's voice began to crack, as if the demon inside him had awakened and drained him of his humanity.

'It was not a wish, Iblis. What made you think it was a wish?' Lucy replied in a flat tone, her anger boiling beneath the surface.

'You have made your first wish,' he repeated, this time in a demonic cry.

'No, I have not. You should have been more careful before granting one, especially if it's important to you.'

'Ah, cunning old Lucy,' the djinn said, his rage intensifying. 'You have managed to trick the King of Djinns, and for that I must pay the price that the lamp demands.'

Iblis stretched out his right hand towards her, revealing a grotesque sight. Lucy saw a decaying finger, riddled with wriggling worms and oozing dark, tar-like blood. He grasped it firmly with his other hand and with a swift, violent motion tore it from his body. The djinn's roar of agony was deafening, causing the ground beneath her feet to tremble. She instinctively clutched her hands over her ears and crouched, trying to protect herself from the monstrous being before her.

13

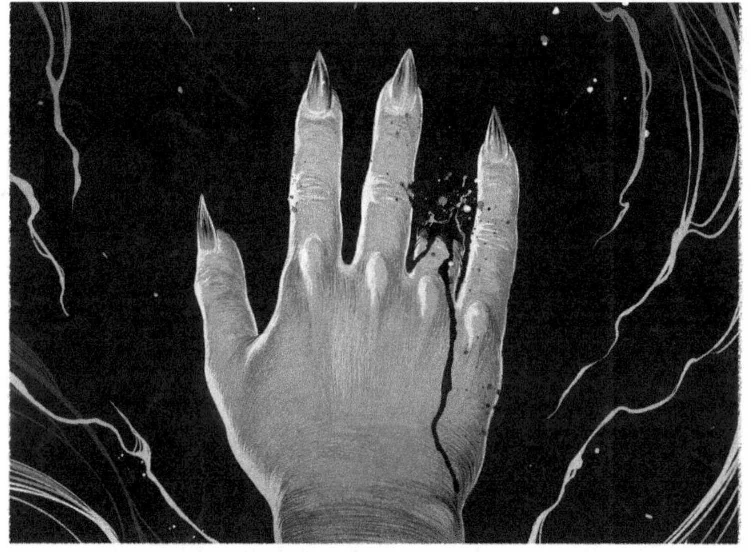

'The pain, the lingering sting of betrayal.'

'What was that?' Lucy inquired, remaining on the floor, her heart racing from the startling revelation. Her initial resentment towards the djinn for unmasking her husband's hidden thoughts had subsided, replaced by an unforeseen compassion upon witnessing his distress.

'Oh, it's nothing,' Iblis replied with a shrug, casually picking up his bloody finger and blowing on it, causing it to disintegrate into dust. The putrid smell of decaying flesh filled the room, making Lucy's eyes water and her nose wrinkle in disgust.

'What is all this, Iblis?' Lucy asked, her voice laced with concern. She felt a mix of fear, anger and guilt, and her heart weighed heavy with sympathy for the stranger who had tried to help her.

'I am the king of djinns, the almighty and powerful,' he answered. 'But the curse still plagues my soul, like barbed wire etched into my body. When the magic trapped me in the lamp, it commanded me never to grant wishes unless asked by my master.'

'So?'

'So, no free wishes, Lucy,' Iblis replied, laughing like a child. 'Or I go back to the dust that I came from, deteriorating slowly and steadily without goodbyes. This time it was a finger, next time it might be my ears or my tail. A djinn without his tail is like a rabid dog in the world of gods.'

'I didn't know.' Lucy's voice was tinged with gloom.

'You see this?' Iblis leaned in closer to her, directing her attention to his left eye. She observed its pallid hue, akin to lifeless flesh.

'Once I granted a wish against death herself. And in return, the lamp asked for my eye. I had to give it without hesitation.' He spoke with a voice laden with sorrow and regret. 'With it, I lost a portion of my power. I became a shell of my former self, suffering silently in the darkness.'

Iblis paused for a moment, his expression pensive.

'Without eyes, we are lost in this world of endless energy,' he continued. 'Like a kite in a storm, thrown around by the winds, without any sense of direction or control.'

'Djinns have problems too?'

'Oh, Lucy, we all have problems, we all suffer in our own ways—humans, djinns, demons, the gods. It's a fundamental aspect of existence, there is no running away from it,' he went on, his voice trembling with a rare display of vulnerability. 'And yet, it is through this very suffering that we would find ourselves, all of us, in our own ways and dimensions.'

'What can I do to ease your pain?' Lucy instinctively asked, her gaze fixed on his bright right eye. Behind the delicate veil of his iris, an intricate world of pulsating colours materialised—red, blue and violet lines of light weaved a hypnotic tapestry, the smallest of creatures crawled and coalesced in a never-ending dance of creation. Mammals, avians and reptiles moved in elegant unison, forming celestial patterns that resembled constellations. Then there were stars, countless, bright and yellow, intertwined to create galaxies beyond measure, encompassing worlds that defied description. Beyond its endless chasms of infinity moved a perfect sphere of a comet with the dark hues of opal.

At its centre, an ethereal castle loomed, and upon a throne within it sat Iblis, his graceful fingers caressing a glowing orb, revealing moving images of humanoid beings walking and talking.

The sight overwhelmed Lucy, its mystical allure captivating her in a haunting, seductive way. Her stomach churned, and she felt as though she might soon throw up.

'Aah, look at you, summoning magic at your whim and peering into a djinn's thoughts,' Iblis commented.

'Summoning or not, I am not a big fan of slipping into the unknown. How do I opt out of this?' asked Lucy, visibly agitated. She jumped to her feet and started stretching her arms. The sensation of nausea grew stronger. Her body felt like it was fresh out of a roller-coaster ride, stomach turned and legs and arms frozen with fear. *Breathe, just breathe. Take long, long breaths,* she told herself.

'No one is a fan of insanity, Lucy. But just because you don't like it doesn't mean it won't happen again. Magic always finds its way to those it deems worthy.'

Lucy hurried to the bathroom, bracing herself to vomit. She dropped to her knees on the spotless white floor in front of the European-style toilet, her head hovering just above the opening.

'I heard you ask if there's any way to ease my pain.' Iblis transformed into a solemn scholar from ancient Greece, garbed in a knee-length blue woollen tunic and a white linen toga draped over his left shoulder.

'Before we even consider how to alleviate someone's pain, we should first ask ourselves: what is pain?' Iblis said. 'Is it not just a construct of our shared imagination? I am not saying that losing a finger isn't painful—that's certainly no laughing matter. I'm referring to the thoughts that come after the injury, the ones that make you feel as though you deserve the punishment from forces you never knew existed. What did I do to deserve this? you ask. Is it to be trapped in a lamp and made to be a slave to mortals whom I despised so much?' Iblis clasped his leather belt, adorned with gold and silver studs, and moved gracefully in his sandals. 'But there are other ways to look at it, one that fills my heart with a sense of purpose. Why can't all this be a path towards divinity, a journey of self-discovery and rebirth that transcends boundaries of consciousness? Aren't we all stiving to be something greater than ourselves?'

'You are not helping,' she said, staring into the shiny depths of the water closet. Her stomach growled again. 'I am not in the mood for puzzles, Iblis. Can we talk about something else?'

'There are no puzzles to be solved, Lucy. No new codes to crack,' Iblis declared, raising his chin like a marble statue in a museum. 'Pain, if viewed in the right light, is neither unbearable nor eternal. It has its limits, and it can serve a purpose. Sometimes, it is even better than meaningless pleasure. What matters most is how you perceive it. Your soul takes on the colour of your thoughts.'

'So, you're saying that you're happy, perfectly content in that lamp?'

'No, no, no, who told you that?' Iblis replied with a grin. 'I'm no god on the path to divinity. I'm just a borderline depressed djinn who wants an escape. But I too have my fair share of oxymoronic thoughts.' He started to chuckle.

'What do you really want, Iblis? Stop fooling around!'

'Make a wish, Lucy,' Iblis said, his voice taking on a slow, dark and commanding tone. 'I am a djinn, and you are my master. Your wish is my command, and it is only through you that I can be freed. And what is more beautiful than freedom?'

The sound of his slow-moving words sliced through Lucy like a knife, causing her to shudder—a stark reminder that she was dealing with an otherworldly entity, one whose very essence was cloaked in an aura of mystery.

During that ephemeral instant between her revelations, Lucy caught another glimpse of his dark, shrewd and untamed mind. Iblis reclined majestically on his throne, hands gliding over his curved crimson horns.

A deep-rooted sense of isolation and yearning enveloped him. Lucy could sense the weight of the curse that bound him to his lamp and the pain he had endured for centuries. Despite the treachery and frailties of his past masters, he still adored them. They were what he thought of.

'Love is all he ever wanted,' she whispered to herself.

At the same time, she was forced to confront the spectres of her own loneliness and despair. Without warning, they took her back to her college days, where she sat alone in a corner of her classroom, consumed by the futility of existence. Throughout those bleak years, the thought of ending her life was her only constant companion.

Jumping from the rooftop of the women's hostel, imagining the wind whipping past her face as she fell, or hanging from a fan, envisioning the slow suffocation that would overtake her as she struggled for breath—these were fantasies that excited her.

During those days, she carried a blade and often thought about the release it would bring if she used it.

Even though life was not harsh on a day-to-day basis, her memories made her future unbearable. She felt sad for no reason—it was sort of dreadful melancholy that reminds one of decay and disorder.

Then like a beacon of hope, Adityan entered her life. When they met for the first time, he was dressed in a crisp white T-shirt and blue jeans, his hair neatly combed to the side. He wasn't the most striking man she had ever laid eyes on, but when he stepped into the classroom his radiance filled up the entire space. She could not see anyone but him. When their eyes met, words evaporated, and thoughts moved freely. They were two souls destined to complete one another. *Without him, what was the point of anything?*

'I can see what you see, Lucy. But I should warn you that not all you remember is true. Sometimes memories deceive you, for they too are nothing but a construct of your imagination,' Iblis said in a measured tone.

'What I want is love, my djinn. That is all that I want,' she declared, rising from the floor and fixing him with a determined stare. 'Take me back in time. Help me relive my past. There are things I must set right. That is my wish.'

'As you wish, master,' Iblis replied, humming a tune.

The room started shaking violently and Lucy's hands and legs grew numb. 'Turning back time comes at a price, Lucy. You can't relive it all. I'll grant you three days and three chances to revisit your past. But remember, no matter how hard you try, you can't alter your present.'

Lucy nodded in disappointment. 'Now, close your eyes and return to where you belong. Before you know, you will become!' said Iblis.

14

When Lucy opened her eyes again, it felt like she had been asleep.

Thanks to Raghavendra Bhattacharya's sharp aim, the white chalk hit right on her forehead and she was awake. For a few seconds, Lucy didn't know where she was but then she noticed the entire class staring at her.

'Are you sleeping in my class?' the professor shouted, gripping another piece of chalk in case he needed to make a second attempt. 'Just because you sit at the back, don't think you can hide from me. This is the last time I will tolerate such disrespectful behaviour from you,' he warned.

'Sorry, sir, I'm not sure what happened, I was ...' she said, quickly straightening up. Raghavendra returned to the blackboard and continued writing lines from Kabir's verses. Lucy strained to decipher the text:

Kasturi kundali base, mrig dhoondhe ban maahi
Aise ghati ghati Ram hae, duniya dekhi naahi

'The poem highlights our tendency to seek happiness and fulfilment externally, when in reality, true joy and satisfaction come from within. Kabir emphasises that both divinity and spiritual wisdom exist within us, and the path to self-realisation involves discovering and embracing this inner light. The sun serves as a metaphor for the divine or ultimate truth, which, although it may seem distant, shines upon our lives and offers guidance. The process of spiritual growth and self-realisation takes time to unfold, and it's crucial to remain connected to our inner selves, without being influenced by the material world's illusions.' The professor strolled through the room, ensuring his students were engaged.

Poets have always carried a certain air of hypocrisy, speaking as though they understand everything and setting lofty expectations for ordinary people, Lucy thought discontentedly while her gaze returned to the back of her notebook where she resumed drawing doodles.

Among the haphazardly sketched illustrations, her round face appeared, surrounded by turbulent clouds and rain—an introspective depiction of her depression. In the margins, there were drawings of men, whose eyes, lips, broad chests and strong legs she had highlighted. Although she longed to find such men, she felt undeserving of their attention.

'As I will be retiring at the end of this semester, I have chosen to pass on my classes to Adityan Roy, the new visiting lecturer in our department. He is an outstanding academic and is presently working towards his PhD in Digital Art.' Raghavendra's commanding voice pulled her back from her reverie.

A man in a white full-sleeved T-shirt and blue jeans walked in. His flat belly and freshly shaved baby face put an instant smile on the faces of most women in the class. Lucy looked at his bright brown eyes, and they looked back at her. Her cheeks reddened. She felt seen.

Fifteen minutes into the lesson, Lucy was struck by a powerful sense of déjà vu. It wasn't merely that this had happened before, but she knew what would transpire next. Memories of the class and the man lingered in her heart. She knew him. She knew the course their relationship would take. Her feet grew cold and her hands dampened with sweat. She feared she was on the verge of a psychotic episode.

Why do I feel like this? she wondered.

Remember the wish … the wish, a cold tune arrived at the right time. She suddenly remembered the djinn and the day she had chosen. 'I remember,' she replied.

This is how going back in time feels like, like you're waking up from a dream in a state of uncertainty and self-doubt. But that does not change the fact that you are reliving your past, the day of your choice. Now, let's see who he is, the man who took your heart. Let us dive into his deepest desires, his thoughts, his intentions. At that instant, Lucy could not separate herself from the djinn. It was like they were one mind in the same body.

Like a finely tuned antenna receiving invisible signals, Lucy suddenly became conscious of the abundant thoughts drifting and intermingling in the air around her. The critical, analytical, creative, self-indulging spectrum of non-stop conversations. She felt like a child who had just seen a rainbow for the first time.

Boys sitting behind her pondered over cricket matches, while a girl nearby daydreamed about Shah Rukh Khan. Another's stomach rumbled with hunger, and someone else longed to jump upon their desk and release a wild howl. The thoughts of others seemed to have a life of their own. She could hear their voices accompanying them. Elusive and dynamic, they defied control and understanding. Among the luminous, pure and virtuous thoughts, there lurked darker, sinister whispers too.

The afterglow, focus on that, they all have it—these transient thoughts vanish as quickly as they emerge. 'Seize them before they disappear,' the djinn commented, giving her instructions on how to tune herself to the new world of energy. 'Like fireflies who cannot be caught, their luminescence will wane and vanish if you don't focus.'

'Excuse me, are you Lucy?' A hand fell on her desk.

'Yes, yes. I am Lucy … Lucy David,' she replied, breaking away from her thoughts.

'Granddaughter of the famous Zacharia Cheriyan from Kerala, right?'

'Aaaah, yes … How did you know?'

'Vasu, your history teacher. He's from Kerala, and he mentioned your family owns the *Daily Malayalam*,' Adityan stated, spreading both his hands over the bench and fixing his gaze on her. Without effort, fragments of his thoughts started whistling at her.

She's not as pretty as Vasu described, too skinny and a bit dark. Just look at that sad face and the oily hair. Why do girls use so much oil? She doesn't appear so posh; maybe it's all under the clothes.

'Excuse me?'

'Did I say something wrong? What happened?' Adityan asked in his calm, sweet voice.

'Nothing, I just thought I heard something,' she replied, her mind drawn back to the vivid thoughts emanating from the young man as he spoke to her.

His thoughts resembled static images, their edges and corners blurred, reminiscent of a painter who left faces undefined. However, an underlying lucidity rendered everything comprehensible. His mental ruminations mirrored him—cryptic, obscure and unrestrained.

Beneath the facade of innocent eyes and a cherubic grin, she discerned a shrewd, older soul meticulously planning each move in life's grand game. Much like a chess grandmaster, he was a relentless strategist who could artfully navigate any challenge. She could now sense the workings of a cunning sociopath concealed beneath his youthful charm.

Lucy ventured deeper into the recesses of Adityan's recollections, unearthing episodes from his past where he ensnared women and manipulated them to satisfy his desires. He never felt love, just an abundance of lust and dominance. As she sought to uncover his true essence and the secrets of his heart, she found herself unable to penetrate beyond his superficialities.

Lucy unearthed his steadfast belief: There's no greater power than a man with money—they break rules and don't fear tomorrow. They're society's puppeteers, dictating its fate. And as she followed its inception, she saw women, both young and old, longing for Adityan's attention, captivated by his masterful seduction. With an air of elegance, he made them feel desired, all the while seeking to boost his own status.

'Hey, Lucy, you still with me?' Adityan snapped his fingers near her face, pulling her back to reality.

'You're a devious man, full of manipulation and deceit. How did I not see it before?' Lucy snapped.

'What?'

What did this bitch just call me? Devious? Just look at her face—pitiful, repulsive, grease smeared over her eyes. If not for the grandfather's money, no one would have bothered to look at that ugly ...

'Enough! I don't need you to tell me I'm ugly. I know who I am,' Lucy shouted at the man, silencing the entire class.

Adityan's face turned red. He felt naked, exposed.

'I am done with you and your two-faced ways,' Lucy shouted as she threw her book to his face and ran towards the door. At the back of her mind, she murmured in anger: 'Get me out of this shithole, I've had enough, let me go back.'

15

That morning, Lucy was awakened by an unexpected call. 'Appapan' came up on the screen, with Zacharia's face dancing to the ringtone.

They would speak every Sunday after church, but that had stopped since Susanna fell ill six months ago. In a dream the previous night, Lucy found herself at Palathikal House, sipping tea with her grandmother. They discussed the reasons behind her reluctance to return home after leaving for school, and she confessed that it was all due to Zacharia.

'After you fell sick with Huntington's disease, grandfather has been acting strange,' she complained.

'Strange how?' Susanna inquired.

'I think, it started with Appapan deciding to pay for renovating Vallarpadam Basilica. Then he brought preachers home to pray for you. They told him that maybe the sickness was a punishment from God since he started getting involved in superstitions and witchcraft.'

'Superstition and witchcraft?'

'Apparently, Appapan told a priest that he got a strange lamp and believes he's hearing voices from it. He's concerned it might be against the Bible,' Lucy whined.

'Oh, it is not that,' Susanna smiled. 'Zacharia is depressed. That's what happens when you love something so dearly and it decides to leave.'

Lucy acknowledged her grandmother with an indifferent nod. She understood her grandmother's message but found herself powerless to help. As the dream neared its end, Susanna confided in Lucy that her time was drawing near and asked her to meet Zacharia more frequently. And then Lucy drifted back to sleep.

'Appappa, what's going on?' Lucy pressed the answer button, her voice tinged with disinterest.

'Lucy … I have terrible news.' Zacharia sounded like he had been crying. She sensed the impending revelation before he could share the news out loud. But to her own surprise, she felt nothing—no sorrow or shock, no dismay or despair. It was just another day.

'Book a flight as soon as you can and come here,' Zacharia urged. Lucy responded with a drawn-out 'Hmm' betraying her reluctance to return home and confront the memories of the loss of her parents. Heavy silence enveloped them before Zacharia ended the call.

'Who is it? And this early in the morning?' someone asked, wrapping their arms around her from behind.

'Zacharia Appapan called. Ammamma has passed away,' Lucy stated flatly, seemingly untroubled.

Adityan's eyes widened. 'Maybe you should go … I can come with you, and we can meet your family,' he suggested, rising from the bed to search for his T-shirt on the floor. *Finally, Mr Zacharia and I can discuss some business!*

'Business?'

'What business? I just said maybe we should go together,' Adityan said quickly. He found his T-shirt, got dressed, and hurried to the small kitchen to make his morning coffee.

Lucy stretched her arms, adjusted her hair and hopped off the bed. However, she lost her footing and tumbled to the floor. A torrent of memories, faces and events washed over her. Sitting up, she crossed her legs and placed her hands over her head. *What is this sensation? Why do I feel like this has happened before?*

.... *the wish,* a voice emerged from the depth of her gut, and with it came an astonishing clarity. Suddenly, everything became crystal clear. 'Oh shit, oh shit,' she screamed, panicking over her realisation.

Looking into the mirror beside the bed, she observed her once-vibrant hair with its awkward fringe. There were no dark circles, no wrinkles and no melancholic frown.

'What is it? Tickets are booked out?' Adityan entered the room holding a cup of coffee.

'Nothing … nothing.'

Neither the past nor the already unfolded present can be altered. But by making other choices, one can delve into the unexplored and uncover the emotional landscapes they unveil, she heard someone whisper in her ear.

'But why this day?' Lucy tried to remember what she had done when this day had come around for the first time.

That day, too, she woke up to her grandfather's call and Adityan mentioned booking tickets. But the tickets were never booked, and she didn't even leave the apartment. In hindsight, that was the reason Zacharia never talked to her again.

From there, things were never the same and she lost touch with her family. And somehow, as if the older version of herself grew enough to understand things with maturity, actions of her past were given a new perspective.

Susanna had been a constant presence in her life and had moulded Lucy into the person she eventually became. How could she even fathom missing her grandmother's funeral? But she hadn't been emotionally equipped to confront her grandmother's passing, and was too young to comprehend that people leave this world not to inflict pain but as a part of life's voyage.

Overwhelmed by shame and guilt, tears streamed down Lucy's face. *Why didn't I offer her my final respects?* Compelled by the weight of her emotions, she swiftly booked the next available flight and hastily filled two small suitcases.

16

'All should return to where we began.'

The afternoon Air India flight landed in Kochi around 3 p.m. As Lucy and Adityan exited the airport, she spotted an older man with a white beard and sparkling bald head holding a board that read 'Lucy David'.

'Hello, Paulose etta, here … here.' She waved her hands in an attempt to be seen.

Within a minute, Paulose, the family driver, was beside them, carrying their luggage. The short, stout man with an overly wide smile appeared taken aback to see a North Indian man accompanying Lucy. *Kollam, fair and tall. Looks like some Bollywood actor. Zacharia sir might like him.* Paulose made some quick judgements in his mind, and his murmurs made their way to Lucy.

She smiled widely, thinking about how odd it was to listen to people's thoughts.

On their way to Palathikal House, Paulose shared the local news and family gossip. 'Everyone is telling Zacharia sir to remarry, especially Elza molae. I think America changed her. She says everyone there marries someone as soon their wife dies. A strange country, right?' Paulose said jokingly.

They don't want to take care of him, cunning bastards. Just like all other spoilt brats, all they want to do is smile and talk sweetly so they can get all his money. Raising children is such a waste now. The inner monologues always came as background clangour.

On the short trip from the airport to Palathikal House, Lucy learnt more about Paulose than she had during the eighteen years she had spent in his presence. She understood that behind his calm and poised smile lay a frustrated man who hated people for everything they did.

Upon Lucy's arrival, the most excited was Tipu, who barked violently for her attention. As soon as the door swung open, Lucy jumped out of the car and ran towards his cage. 'Tipu, Tipu baby, how are you doing, my darling?' She grabbed his face through the steel bars. The pup ceased his tantrums and began to squeal with excitement.

Though she could not read the animal's thoughts, she could feel the warmth, the adoration, the love that flowed out of his body. It made her feel euphoric. Tipu wrestled his face out of her hands and Lucy lost her balance. She fell and lost consciousness.

'Chee … must have caused an allergy or something,' Adityan ran towards her and pulled her up. He looked at the dog furiously, as if the pup had ruined his long-awaited appearance. And in return, the animal started to bark at the devil that hid inside the man.

When Lucy woke up, she was on the sofa. Next to her head sat Zacharia with a palm on her forehead. Opposite them on a chair were her uncle George and his wife Gracy. They were chatting with Adityan, discussing his business strategies and the app's impressive growth rate. In the background played a Christian funeral song, a tune equally melodious and sad.

Maranam varumoru naal orkuka marthya ne
Koode porum nin jeevitha cheythikalum
Salkrithyangal cheyuka ne alasatha koodathe
(Death will come on one day, remember that always.
And with it, your life's actions will be counted.
Do good deeds without hesitation as the chariot arrives
to take you back.)

The song brought back memories Lucy wanted to forget, the one where the remains of her parents lay inside their coffins. Their partially destroyed orifices had been filled with cotton, and their heads meticulously stitched together to prevent them from falling off. Just the thought of it made Lucy's hands shiver.

She wanted a strong drink—whiskey, rum, or even nadan kalle that Zacharia usually kept in the kitchen.

'Aaah, molae, you awake?' asked Zacharia, looking down at her. 'Should I call Dr Kururp? Everything all right?'

'I am okay, Appappa, everything is all right. I just need some fresh air,' she lied. But despite her reluctance to share her thoughts and the belief that Zacharia was incapable of understanding her feelings, she soon heard his delicate inner conversations. It arrived like a gentle gust from the ocean, chilly and strong, like tides brushing against the most hidden corners of her heart.

Zacharia's mind wandered to a long-forgotten memory, one where little Lucy squirmed out of Susanna's hold and sprinted towards her parents, ready to embark on a trip in their vibrant red Jeep. In this memory, her parents' faces were strikingly clear—she could picturise David's rugged beard and Caroline's hair interwoven with delicate lace braids.

As the child reached them, they enfolded her in a warm embrace, peppering her cheeks with tender kisses. They then looked towards Zacharia and hollered, 'Keep an eye on her, and don't let her spend all day in front of the television! We'll be back before you know it!'

'Da, Davidae, she's my granddaughter—you needn't tell me how to make her feel at home. You lovebirds go and enjoy some time off,' Zacharia shouted back. The couple beamed brightly before setting off on their adventure. The old man stood watch; his gaze fixed on the receding car till it became a mere dot on the horizon.

Zacharia's thoughts shifted to another memory—a darker, more painful one. He stood in a morgue, his heart pounding with such ferocity that he struggled to remain upright, as he awaited the doctor's unveiling of the two bodies.

'The accident likely occurred when the driver tried to overtake a truck on a hairpin turn. That's what the police believe. The Nilgiri hills are notorious for accidents,' the doctor shared solemnly, preparing him for what was to come. 'I must warn you, the bodies are in terrible shape, almost unrecognisable—their skulls crushed, their limbs dislocated.'

As the veil was lifted, Zacharia was confronted with the horrific sight of two mangled forms. He collapsed to his knees, the weight of the scene too much to bear. *Oh God, why have you brought this upon us? Where will I find the words to share this with their child?*

In that instant, Lucy could feel the immense burden of sorrow that forever haunted Zacharia. The devastating experience had ignited a deep, unshakeable fear of death within him. The gruesome sight he had been forced to confront sent him spiralling into depression. He became consumed by a fear of losing more loved ones, and it felt as if a part of his sanity had been stolen away.

'Go see Susanna, she is in the living room,' Zacharia informed, tapping Lucy back to the room. 'Elza's husband will get here only tomorrow morning. Flights from the USA are not easy to catch, she says. So we planned the funeral for tomorrow morning.'

Lucy nodded, a sense of relief washing over her as she realised that after midnight, she would finally be released from this day and able to move on to something less burdensome. Rising from the sofa, she scanned the assembled crowd of relatives, cousins and neighbours with anxious eyes, seeking familiar faces. Spotting none, she gripped Adityan's wrist, leading him to the main hall where Susanna's body was resting in a coffin.

'Everyone had a lot of questions—about where we met, how long it has been, what I do,' Adityan informed her enthusiastically, 'and somehow in the middle of all that I managed to get an appointment with Mr George, your uncle. He is a sharp businessman, wanted to invest in our company.'

'Oh, okay,' Lucy nodded, uninterested.

Upon entering the stately chamber, redolent with the scent of fresh marigolds and incense sticks, her eyes fell upon her grandmother's countenance—pale, desiccated and unmistakably lifeless. It was evident that her spirit had departed, no longer tethered to the mortal confines of her corporeal form.

'Ammamma, I am sorry I was not around,' Lucy murmured, trying to ease off the uncomfortable feeling that was threatening to overwhelm her.

The memories of their cherished moments together swirled in her mind, evoking an intense longing for the past. It felt as if everything had happened just yesterday. 'I wish I had more time with you,' she complained.

Lucy gazed at the people encircling the casket and noticed the sympathy in their eyes. They silently extended their support, refraining from passing any judgement at this emotionally charged time.

But Adityan had all sorts of thoughts.

This coffin must have cost a fortune. Just look at that gold trim, must be teakwood. These people have money to burn. I need to make sure I meet Mr Zacharia before I leave. Adityan's thoughts hung in the air like a foul smell.

How did I end up with him? She moved her eyes to the kitchen; she desperately needed a drink.

17

Lucy couldn't recall how much alcohol she had consumed the previous day. Her head was throbbing as if it had been struck by a club. When she opened her eyes, she found herself at Vallarpadam Basilica, listening to the funeral mass by Father Kurian.

A nostalgic familiarity enveloped her as she surveyed the church's interiors; they had remained largely unaltered since her childhood. Lucy struggled to discern whether it was the resonating hum of prayers, the solemn faces of the mourners or the lingering hangover that churned her stomach with a sickening unease.

Why am I still here? she thought, grinding her teeth. *Iblis, answer me.* There was no response. She couldn't hear anyone else's thoughts either.

Seated beside her on the wooden bench in the front row, Zacharia rested his hand on hers. His cold skin sent shivers down her spine. The sheer intensity of emotions in the church left her feeling overwhelmed. She recalled going to the kitchen the night before, grabbing a bottle of rum and heading for the terrace with a tub of ice. She drank, cried, looked at the stars and wondered why they always look down on others. And then there was Iblis, warning her not to drink. They talked about how alcohol, drugs and misdeeds can disrupt a person's connection to the divine.

What happened after that? She didn't remember. *How did I get here? Was it all just a drunken dream? Zacharia's death, the lamp and the djinn?*

'It is time to go to the burial ground,' Zacharia tapped her softly on her cheek. Lucy rose to her feet and gave a slight nod.

Father Kurian and his helper guided the pallbearers to their destination behind the church. They prayed and sprinkled holy water from the church's entrance to the burial site located in the heart of the cemetery. The crowd followed in unison.

But even in a moment of great despair, there was a sense of pride as they approached the family's private marble-covered burial plot. The shiny headstones stood as a symbol of status and wealth among the plainer graves of the other deceased.

'They have a marble-glazed place to rest, not the cheap concrete,' Lucy heard one of the mourners murmurs. 'Look at the decoration, the fresh roses, lilies and jasmine flowers. Even in death, the rich go lavishly.'

The crowd came to a halt in front of a six-foot deep, freshly dug pit. The men tied ropes to the sides of the casket and waited for the family to give Susanna their final kiss before lowering it.

In succession, the close family members approached the coffin to say their final goodbyes. Zacharia was the first, then George, Gracy, Elza and her husband. Then everyone looked at Lucy, and, as if controlled by those gathered, her legs moved on their own and she came face to face with her dead grandmother. Lucy took a deep breath and silenced her thoughts.

I am happy to see you, Lucy. I always wondered why you never came back to give me a kiss, she heard her grandmother's voice as her lips touched Susanna's forehead. Lucy bounced up and went back to join the others.

Calm your mind, Lucy, calm it down, another feeble voice followed. Lucy inhaled deeply. Suddenly, as if a knot had been undone, she could hear the lost voices of others. They weren't as clear as before though.

Lucy, I told you not to indulge in anything that could disturb your focus. If you drink, you lose your body's ability to tune into me and others, she heard a warning, but Iblis's voice seemed distant and faint. Lucy grew more agitated, as she had many questions to ask him.

After the funeral, the crowd left the burial ground together. George invited the priest and helpers to join him for an evening meal at his home. Zacharia asked Lucy to ride with him in his Benz and instructed Paulose to take the day off.

As they drove to Palathikal House, the old man tried to make a conversation with his granddaughter.

'How is life, molae?'

'Good, Appappa.'

'You never told me that you met someone.'

'I thought you wouldn't like him.'

'When was the last time I said no to anything that you wanted, Lucy?' Zacharia's voice got serious. 'But, molae, something about him is not right, he is not who he pretends to be.'

'He is a good man, Appappa,' she said instinctively.

'Listen to me closely, my dear child. I am an old man; I have seen all sorts of men in my time. Men who give their hearts, men who want to protect the weak, men who only care about themselves. And this man you're involved with falls into the last category. I'm not saying he'll hurt you now, but mark my words, his intentions are not pure. He's not interested in you for who you are. He cares about the money and status of our family. And sooner or later, he will reveal his true nature,' Zacharia said grumpily, his eyes locked on hers. 'Last night, during a time of mourning, he had the audacity to ask me to invest in your company. A man who talks about money during a funeral has a heart far from good. He's not here to serve but to take. So, I urge you, my dear, be careful.'

18

The afternoon light filtered through the large windows and illuminated the room. Lucy lay on the floor, orienting herself to the new reality of her life. The sight of the blue sofa and the double bed with fresh linen confirmed that the wish had ended, and she was back in her hotel room.

With effort, Lucy rose from the floor and made her way to the washroom to freshen up. Memories swirled around her mind like paper boats in the monsoon rain. But they slowly drifted away as she adjusted to her new surroundings. Lucy was reluctant to let them go, she knew she had lessons to learn from them. She summoned her remaining focus to hold on to those events so they wouldn't be forgotten like a fleeting dream.

In the full-length mirror in the washroom, she stared at herself. Her hair was back to its usual form—boring black and long. As expected, the dark circles and frown returned too, and she gasped in disappointment. After fixing her clothes and brushing her teeth, Lucy returned to the room. *Where is my phone? There might be messages from the bank, possibly from the lawyer,* she kept thinking, but her tired feet led her to the bed.

'Would you care for something to eat?' Iblis appeared by her side dressed as a butler. He looked surprisingly debonair in his tailored blue suit and bow tie, except for the pointed tail that flicked behind him. 'How was your trip down memory lane? Was it as delightful as you had hoped?' he jeered with a hint of sarcasm.

'For a moment, I thought I would never see you,' Lucy complained.

'Oh, that. Yes, of course. Lucy, it's important to know that not everyone can see or hear me, no matter how hard they try. And just because you're able to perceive me at this moment doesn't guarantee that you'll be able to do so in the future.'

'Why?'

'Why? Because not everyone is born equal, though one would like to believe that is the case. Not everyone's heart is pure enough to catch the magic that surrounds them anew.' Iblis approached her, extending his palm.

Within its grasp, she beheld a mesmerising display of planets, stars and cosmic clouds, all swirling and twinkling in a beautiful cosmic dance. The vibrant hues of red, blue and green filled the expanse before her, as she felt herself drawn deeper into the infinite mystery of the universe.

'Life flows like a river, ever-changing, short-lived yet vibrant, a mere flicker in the grand scheme. We all live forever, yet we forget.'

'I don't understand.'

'In the vast expanse of the universe, you are but a star, a spark of cosmic dust, through lives and worlds. You journey forth, carrying the weight of actions past.' The projections inside his palm changed again, revealing the metamorphosis of a larva into an insect. 'You began as a fleeting mayfly, living for but a day, and as you pondered your existence and purpose, the weight of such musings became too heavy for your being to bear, leading to death and rebirth. Then you were a rat, not a smart one, but one who took care of its young. And that too passed through the cycle of thoughts, death and rebirth. This went on forever and ever, from insects to mammals, to plants, to humans. Upon mastering life's lessons, ascension continues—as a river bestowing life's sweet embrace, as a vigilant mountain with wisdom and grace, then as a planet who cradles and nourishes, and finally as stars. Then after all that is done, you open your eyes as a lost djinn, a God, maybe universe itself.'

'As rivers, mountains and planets? Gods and djinns?' Lucy asked, her eyes wide in disbelief.

'Despite your inability to communicate with them, their existence is undeniable. Like you, they too have set forth on a profound pilgrimage for truth, commencing from the depths of ignorance and gradually gaining wisdom through life's teachings. It is within the intricate weave of innumerable lifetimes that you, as a seeker of wisdom, can begin to unveil the grandiosity that binds us all.'

'I don't understand much. Do you mean reincarnations?'

'You are getting there,' Iblis laughed loudly. 'You've journeyed through many forms and shapes, in countless bodies through the ages, to get to this moment. Your true age surpasses comprehension, for you are the eternal energy that traverses the span of time.'

'What does all this have to do with your disappearance?'

'One's body and mind should be refined to catch the vibrations that float around. They are attainable only through the experiences of past lives. Don't forget that you were able to sense the thoughts of others, these were frequencies inaudible to mortals.' Iblis kept his left palm on his chest. 'For I am but a mere vibration, heard by only the pure of heart. The more you numb your senses with the vices of pride, greed, lust, envy, gluttony, wrath and sloth, the more my presence thou shalt discern.'

'For a king of djinns, you talk a lot of shit,' Lucy smiled widely. 'So you never spoke to my grandfather?'

'Zacharia never laid eyes on me. Neither did he summon my presence nor was he granted wishes. Not all can master a djinn,' Iblis's voice thickened. 'But I whispered in his ear, guiding him, so you and me would meet in the grand design of fate.'

'Why? Why me?'

'A djinn is a creature of desire, Lucy, and it needs to fall in love with its master to grant them wishes. It is their responsibility to free their master as they liberate themselves.' Iblis gracefully lifted himself into the air, hands folded and chest puffed with pride. His eye danced with a brilliant green light and his teeth grew sharper. 'Now it is time for another wish. What is it that your heart seeks next?'

Lucy lowered her head for a few minutes, thinking about things Iblis had spoken about. She felt overjoyed to hear the phrase 'fall in love', but the memory of the one who had toyed with her emotions swiftly resurfaced. Her body stiffened and her palms grew clammy with sweat. *How dare he play with my heart? How dare Adityan disrespect my grandparents?* She clenched her teeth.

'Revenge is what I seek, Iblis, everything paid back in full.'

'Out of all those things in the world, you choose revenge?' Iblis grinned. 'What can come out of that but meaningless pride?'

'I can't let it pass. It is what I want.'

'All actions have consequences, all choices come with a price. Bear that in mind,' Iblis warned. 'Allow me, if you will, to spin a yarn—a cautionary tale that may change your mind—of a king who paid his dues in time.' The television in the room flickered to life abruptly, and after a few moments of a black and white grainy filter, images of an infant started playing on it.

19

'When I first met Alexander, he was a newborn to his parents, King Philip II of Macedon and Queen Olympias of Epirus. It was fate that brought me there at the exact time of his birth,' Iblis whispered to Lucy. Images of the ancient capital of Macedon, Pella, and its inhabitants began appearing on the television.

'At the time of Alexander's birth, King Philip II was consolidating his power in Macedon and expanding the kingdom's territory through military conquest. As word of the new heir's birth spread, gifts began arriving from all over the region. Gold and ivory came from neighbouring rulers, while merchants gifted gems and silver. But the lamp arrived from a seafarer who was sent by the king to find new trade routes with faraway kingdoms.

'Your Majesty, during our time in the Red Sea we faced wild winds and monstrous waves that nearly took us under. We were fishing for sustenance when, by some twist of fate, we discovered this extraordinary artefact shimmering on the water's surface. It seemed to possess a mystical power that revitalised our spirits and helped us endure nature's fury. At night, I was kept awake by visions of presenting this treasure to you, and now here we are in your esteemed palace,' the seafarer recounted to the king the tale of how he unearthed the extraordinary object.

'Though King Philip II was not particularly superstitious, he felt the lamp's magic upon touch. He kept it in the royal chamber next to his stone Kline.

'Growing up, Alexander was a child of great ambition. Regardless of his rich upbringing, he desired greatness from the very beginning of life. It was that thirst for power and discipline that got my attention.

'By then, I had been under the ocean for more than a thousand years, and the isolation had silenced me. Despite my constant urge to escape captivity, I never reached out to the king or anyone in the palace. Upon encountering Alexander, I wondered why fate brought us together. Although I was hesitant to place my trust in anyone, I began speaking to the child in his sleep, guiding him through dreams.

'Another decade passed before a moment presented itself for us to meet face to face. On that day, King Philip II was assassinated by a man named Pausanias at a public event. Chaos erupted in the streets, spreading rumours of a mutiny. The twenty-year-old Alexander sat next to his father's dead body, not knowing what to do.

'At the right time, a whisper came to his ears, informing him about forces turning against the royal family. "Men seek your demise, their sights set on the throne. They will ruthlessly slaughter your family. Your blood will dampen the arid earth, and your memory will vanish as the next ruler assumes power," the voice murmured.

'"However, I can assist you. Quickly go to your father's quarters and find me on the stone Kline. Without hesitation, open the enchanted lamp, and I shall ensure your safety."

'The young man took the message as a divine intervention from the heavens. He ran as fast as he could and opened the lamp.

'When Alexander first saw me, he was terrified and fell back on the floor. I was in my primitive form—a humongous snake with three animal heads. Out of fear, he cried for me to go back to the lamp. But then he heard the familiar voice, the one from his dreams. It asked him to immediately make a wish to protect himself and his family from the impending danger.

"Protect, both myself and my loved ones, shielding us from those who pursue our harm. May our blood never stain this land," he wished, keeping his eyes closed.

'In an instant, the air before the palace crackled with heat as an inferno roared to life, its voracious flames lapping at the sky like the very jaws of Hades. The intensity of the blaze drew the onlookers to it with the same fatal allure that calls moths to a flame.

'Men and women, consumed by an irresistible urge, ran towards the conflagration, their hearts pounding with every frantic step. The searing heat failed to deter them, and they leaped into the flames with an unnerving abandon, their bodies offered up as unwitting sacrifices.

'Their feet seemed to act of their own accord, driven by a force beyond their control. Little did they know that I, the malevolent djinn, had whispered my incantations into their ears, ensnaring their wills and fuelling their blind descent into the fiery abyss.

'From that fateful moment, I seamlessly interwove myself into Alexander's inner circle, assuming the role of his most trusted confidant. Over the ensuing years, I adopted the form of a formidable Molosser, named Peritas, never straying far from my master's side. I continued to influence the course of Alexander's destiny, expertly navigating the murky waters of power and conquest that surrounded us.

'However, upon realising that I would depart once his three wishes were granted, the cunning king chose a different path. He refrained from asking me to fulfil his desires and instead cleverly leveraged my extraordinary foresight to consistently triumph over his foes and broaden his kingdom's reach.

'I was not pleased. I was again a slave—not to the lamp, but to a man.'

20

'As you wish, master.'

Lucy listened and watched the television with intrigue, as Iblis stood next to her.

Alexander's second wish came during the Siege of Tyre, as his army tried to infiltrate the impregnable Phoenician city.

In just a few years, he had shattered the mighty empire under Darius III at the Battle of Issus, leaving Persian rule in tatters. Egypt, too, had fallen under his sway, its vast trade routes now at his command. People started calling him 'Alexander the Great', the one who would rule the world. He felt invincible and pride had taken hold of his heart.

When the king's eyes first fell on Tyre, a small island off the coast of Lebanon, Iblis warned him not to engage in combat with them. 'Oh, my noble king, I fear that your unchecked hunger for power may ultimately bring about a horrific calamity. Innocent lives would be senselessly sacrificed, and their cries will echo through the ages. These events, spawned by your actions, will inexorably lead to your own demise,' he cautioned. But the king did not listen.

At first, Alexander endeavoured to secure the city through diplomatic means; however, the Tyrians remained steadfast in their refusal to bow before an invader. Frustrated and hungry for conquest, Alexander resolved to enforce a relentless blockade upon the city, intending to crush the spirit of its people and claim his prize.

The siege lasted for seven gruelling months, during which the Tyrians put up fierce resistance. They fought with all their might and used their powerful navy to destroy Alexander's men. When the path to victory seemed treacherous and slim, a mutiny started among Alexander's loyal soldiers. They plotted to kill their king while he slept.

Fortunately, Iblis intervened at the right moment and advised Alexander to make his second wish.

'A rebellion brews within your own ranks, spearheaded by the cavalry commanders,' he warned gravely. 'Their numbers are vast, and they've already devised a plot to cut your life short as you slumber. There is no evading this destiny. Use your second wish to shield yourself from their treachery.'

'How dare they? Unleash your wrath upon them; let none survive, for they must learn that to challenge my rule is to court death itself. This is my second wish,' Alexander roared, his rage boiling over.

In the very next moment, chaos erupted just outside Alexander's tent, as his soldiers clashed with one another. Cries of 'traitors to the throne' rang out amongst the din of battle, as steel met steel, and the agonised screams of the wounded filled the air.

Within moments, the ground was littered with the mutilated remains of the fallen and the severed heads of the cavalry commanders and their followers, serving as gruesome testimony to the swift and brutal retribution that had been exacted.

But the bloodshed did not stop there.

When the war was won three weeks later, the invaders threw the elderly into the fire, assaulted the women and forcefully separated children from their mothers. The remaining Tyrians were sent to Persia, Egypt and Alexandria as slaves and sold to the first bidder.

Among the sold was Hiram, the eldest son of Azemilcus, the army general of the Tyrians, who promised to seek revenge against the person responsible for the massacre. He was initially sold to a blacksmith in Persia, where he worked in his forge for five years. During that time, Hiram drew close to his master and assisted him in crafting exceptional swords, which fetched a high price when sold to local landlords.

With Hiram's assistance, the blacksmith amassed a fortune, and in return, the young man earned his long-sought freedom.

With newfound liberty, he embarked on a journey to Babylon, where Alexander was rumoured to dwell in his grand palace.

As part of his elaborate plan to seek revenge, Hiram managed to get hired by the city's leading wine merchant and began working for him as a low-wage labourer.

Initially, he toiled alongside the slaves on the farm, steadily mastering the craft of grape fermentation. He dedicated himself to refining his techniques. And over the course of four years, Hiram produced Babylon's most sought-after wine and gained the merchant's confidence as his foremost winemaker.

While Hiram's revenge simmered in the background, Alexander continued his violent rampage to expand his territory. He solidified his rule in Central Asia, by defeating the local ruler Spitamenes in the Battle of Jaxartes, and even expanded his borders to India, defeating King Porus in the Battle of Hydaspes.

'Alexander, be wary, for power and greed have altered your essence, creating an ever-expanding rift between us. If this carries on, a day will come when my voice can no longer reach you, and I'll be left as a silent observer, a stranger watching from the periphery. I beg you, don't let this come to pass.' Iblis never stopped warning his master.

Yet, the king continued his acts of violence. His victories became grander, marked by excessive vices which gradually disconnected him from the immense power he once held. Iblis soon became a daydream that he once knew.

When Alexander finally returned to Babylon after his long conquest, he was considered a god among his peers. The city was decorated with banners and garlands, and public performances depicting his war efforts were held everywhere. Women, wine and fresh game waited for his attention in the palace.

In the days that followed, Alexander indulged in all of life's pleasures like a madman. Of all the offerings presented to him, his favourite was the exclusive wine created for him by Babylon's top winemaker. He drank and drank till he lost consciousness. Then, as if the prophecy of the djinn had come true, the young king suddenly fell ill. A brain fever. He eventually passed away.

21

By the time Iblis finished his story, the sun had set. Lucy opened the windows of her twelfth-floor suite and stared at the city drenched in a nighttime glow. Her eyes ached, and her mind was tired from the ceaseless shifts of reality thrust upon her. She didn't know what to do with her thoughts and questioned the fabric of her very existence.

In the distance, she saw tall buildings in grey and white with rooms that were lit up. 'Eyyye, anyone there?' she shouted. The noise from the street below drowned hers.

She looked down at the people and cars who shared the road. She could hear their arguments from up here. A chilly wind blew past her and Lucy tied her hair. *Is this real, or is it another one of those dreams I have been having lately?* she wondered.

Contrary to her usual feeling of wanting to hide from crowds, Lucy found herself yearning to venture out this time, compelled by a need to confide in someone the surreal experiences that had been haunting her. The constant stream of otherworldly hallucinations stoked the flames of paranoia within her. Her sense of reality had been disrupted and she was left grappling with an inability to find equilibrium amid the onslaught of these mystifying apparitions.

Pausing for a moment, Lucy cautiously extended one leg out of the window, attempting to gauge the ledge below. As her foot made contact with the concrete surface, she assessed its width and reach. *I could stand there,* she thought.

'CAREFUL!'

'Hush, hush … Iblis. I don't need your advice on this one.' Lucy tightly grabbed the curtains and dropped her other leg. The cold wind blew again, this time stronger. Her hair escaped from the tight grips of the rubber band and covered her face. After a short struggle to gain balance, Lucy managed to sit back on the edge of the window.

'What are you doing?'

'Trying to make sure this is not one of my usual sessions,' Lucy responded, uninterested in Iblis's question. 'You won't understand. You only hang out with kings and queens, the achievers and movers.'

'Kings and queens?'

'Have you ever put yourself in the shoes of that man who lost everything, the one who was sold into slavery? Can you imagine the heartbreak he must have faced when his entire family vanished one day?' Lucy asked, her legs dangling. 'Wasn't he the very hand of justice that life needed? If it wasn't for him, your Alexander would have continued to wreak havoc and eventually retired to a life of luxury.'

'Hand of justice?' Iblis smiled. 'You see, Lucy, there is no justice, no fairness, no equality in this world. It is every man for himself, and it is up to us to create our destiny—be a god, a djinn or a mortal.'

'Forgive and forget? Is that your next advice?' Lucy clenched her teeth in frustration. She remembered Adityan's cunningness, trickery and shrewdness. *I won't let it pass, even if I have to sacrifice my life.*

'Oh, Lucy dear, understand that life is a soul's fine test, a journey where we do our best. You should see beyond the flesh and bone, and realise that everyone is the same as they search for self and purpose.' Iblis moved towards her, gently closing the distance between their faces. 'You should forgive and forget. Do not dwell in the past, life is just a fleeting breeze.'

Iblis placed his hands on Lucy's shoulders, commencing a tender massage. His firm, steady fingers worked their way through her tense muscles, allowing her to relax. As he persisted, Lucy became engulfed in a deluge of memories, as if reliving another person's experiences. These recollections were not her own but those of someone with whom she shared a connection.

In that flash of the past, she was a boy who sat behind his father's Chetak scooter. He held the older man tightly as they navigated the bustling lanes of Mumbai, skilfully avoiding close encounters with passing cars.

'Beta Adityan, in life, there is only one rule: Survive. You need to survive at all costs,' said the man to his child. The little boy nodded in agreement.

In no time, the scooter screeched to a halt next to a humble one-room shack nestled between Dharavi and Bandra Kurla Complex. Instinctively, the young boy seized one of the unassuming white containers placed outside the house and sprinted to the municipal water truck halt. He seamlessly melded into the gathering of hopeful faces, all anticipating the arrival of life-sustaining water in the next few hours.

As he waited, the boy's eyes scanned the chaotic frame—children his age running barefoot through the dusty alleys, a stray dog nosing around a pile of discarded plastic bottles. Vendors yelling out prices for their dirty vegetables, while women with weary faces argued over a few rupees. A cycle rickshaw clattered past, overloaded with scrap metal, while a shiny sedan, a rare sight there, glided by, its windows rolled up tight, sealing off the world outside.

The boy caught a glimpse of a well-dressed family inside, their faces lit with smiles, completely removed from the hardships surrounding them. The stark truth hit him hard—money ruled these streets. It favoured the wealthy while the rest were left to struggle. *How do I get out of this rat race?*

When he finally returned home, his father was already deep into his third glass of homemade Feni. 'Hey, Adi, check the old batch. If it's good to go, drop it with Kaliram Dada at the harbour. And get cracking on the Colmi; I'll join you after finishing this glass.'

The boy innocently nodded.

Not long ago, his old man had shared with him the secrets of concocting a cashew homebrew. He said it was their ticket away from the slum.

Adityan quickly ran through the steps in his head: De-seed the cashew apples and dump them in Colmi. Squish the juice and shape pulp into mounds. Move neero to half-buried kodem. Let the juice ferment. Check for Urrack in old kodems, mix and distil till it becomes Cazulo.

After working till midnight, he took the packed bottles of Cazulo to the nearby shed. Inside, Kaliram Dada and his crew smoked ganja and played carrom. Adityan sat with them and enjoyed a late-night dinner of egg fried rice with red chutney, while listening to the older men chat about smuggled goods and women. As he savoured their leftovers, a particular conversation stuck with him. It was about Kaliram Dada's younger brother who had married a wealthy woman from Bandra Kurla Complex.

'... her daddu is a loaded settu and has gold shops all over Mumbai. He is set for life. Blessed chap!' Kaliram Dada commented.

'But, dadda, she looks like a kauva, bahut kaala hai.'

'Chup, chutiye!' Kaliram took a bottle and pretended to throw it at the man. 'The best way to escape this rat race is to get married to a rich woman. Who cares about looks, haraami? With all that moolah, you can get as many girls as you want.'

The insights that came out of the sloshed men were a revelation for the young boy. *One day I will also become rich, I will marry a wealthy woman and live like a king,* Adityan promised himself.

Like a spinning top that gradually lost its momentum, the visions soon came to an end. Lucy found herself back in the room, sitting on the edge of the window.

'Don't you see, Lucy, that is where he comes from—the past shapes the future. It is the way things are, a natural course of life,' Iblis murmured in her ears, advising her not to take things personally.

'So what? I'm sick of hearing excuses! I had a tough childhood too, but I chose a different path. Everyone should face the consequences of their actions,' Lucy grunted. 'Enough with the advice, just give me what I want!'

'Master, tell me. What is it your heart desires?'

'REVENGE! I wish to take revenge on the man who made a fool of me. I want to live a life of wealth and fame. I want him to see how far I have come and beg for my attention,' she said before taking her hands off the curtain and falling off the ledge. Her body moved effortlessly through the blanket of air towards the concrete pavement.

22

The digital alarm cried at 5.00 a.m. with the pre-recorded message: 'Wake up, Wake up! Rise and shine! Today is a new day full of endless possibilities. You are strong, capable and bright. Trust yourself and your abilities. Approach this day with positivity and an open mind. Remember, you've got this! Have a great day.'

The automatic curtains opened with a sound, letting the early morning light in. Lucy took off her blindfold and stepped onto the wooden floor barefoot; she stretched her neck, palms and elbows with a cat's precision. In the background, speakers started playing an audiobook by Robin Sharma.

'Life's too short to play small with your talents, you were born into the opportunity as well as the responsibility to become legendary. You've been built to achieve masterwork-level projects, designed to realise unusually important pursuits and constructed to be a force for good on this tiny planet. You have it in you to reclaim sovereignty over your primal greatness in a civilisation that has become fairly uncivilised.' The speaker narrated the book with great enthusiasm.

After fifteen minutes of stretching, Lucy entered the expansive open kitchen where her small robotic cleaner was completing its final tasks. She opened the refrigerator and grabbed a bottle of mineral water infused with Himalayan salt, downing half of it in one gulp. With lithe movements, she pivoted towards her coffee maker, choosing a double espresso, all while continuing her joint-loosening exercises.

'Hey, Google, do I have any messages?' she asked the round device mounted on the wall.

'You have twelve missed calls, eight new emails and seven appointments for the day,' the machine answered almost immediately.

'Walk me through them.'

'Eleven missed calls from *Adityan-ex*, one missed call from *Paul*, first email from *Paul@unicrongroup.com* at 21.00 yesterday says: "Hey Lucy, don't forget about tomorrow's next round with the investors, we should hint at the IPO plans." Second email from *Adityan.roy1245@google.com* at 22.00 yesterday says: "Why are you not replying to my messages? We need to talk now!" Third email from *Adityan.roy1245@google.com* at 22.15 yesterday says: "I will sue your ass if you behave like a bitch." Fourth email from *Adityan.roy* ...'

'Skip to my calendar,' Lucy interrupted, not really interested in knowing more about the emails Adityan had sent. *Pathetic, I should sue you for ruining my morning!*

'Team meeting at 8.00 a.m., annual board meeting at 10.00 a.m., interview with *The Hindu* at 11.00 ...'

Lucy took some fresh fruits from the food basket and threw them into the juicer. She added some protein powder and diet supplements before closing the lid.

'... Meeting with new investors at 2.00 p.m., Intervi ...'

For a brief moment, Lucy paused. *Investor meetings, Adityan, interviews*—too many things to handle. A sense of uneasiness settled in her stomach and her heart pounded rapidly. Without a second thought, she opened the kitchen cabinet and took a half-finished bottle of vodka. She measured it with a shot glass and added it to her morning smoothie.

23

In the garage sat a red Audi R8, a matte black Range Rover and her favourite, the blue Porsche. On special occasions like today, Lucy instinctively gravitated towards the latter. Swift, elegant and imbued with a sense of superiority, it bolstered her confidence when she had to face a roomful of staid men in suits.

As she started the car, the sound system flawlessly carried on where the home audio had left off, with Robin Sharma's resonant voice permeating the space.

He talked of the importance of being around only the highest quality and how, in his business, he allows only the top players. 'You can't have an A-level company with C-level performers,' he made the point with impact. His company's strategy was to release only those products that had the potential to disrupt the market. They had to bring value that could change their field. 'My enterprises only offer services that ethically enrich our clients, deliver a breathtaking user experience and breed fanatical followers who couldn't imagine doing business with anyone else.' As Robin Sharma said this, Lucy nodded to herself. *That is just common sense.*

A year had passed since Picasso surpassed 12 million paid subscribers. The journey had been nothing less than remarkable. When Lucy and her ex-husband, Adityan Roy, co-founded the venture, it was an innovative mobile app for artists seeking to sell their work.

Now, eight years later, the company had revolutionised the art world, democratised its access and formed alliances with prestigious auction houses. They now catered to diverse art forms, from mesmerising photography to elaborate clay modelling, asserting their dominance in the billion-dollar industry as India's sole profitable contender.

In the early days, it was Lucy's uncle George who had demonstrated unwavering faith in their nascent digital venture by supporting it financially. He championed the creation of a vibrant brand and media team, propelling their presence across India with eye-catching advertisements in every state. Art students from around the country were drawn to the platform, witnessing its transformation into a digital wonder.

As the platform reached the milestone of one million users, prominent angel investors such as BlueOcean and LetsVenture eagerly joined the fray. Over the next four years, Picasso grew at an exponential rate. In less than five years, the company established thousands of physical centres throughout India that showcased high-end exhibitions. With celebrities endorsing their brand and sponsoring events across Asia, Picasso's influence continued to expand.

However, despite their meteoric rise, the founders found themselves entangled in a media storm following their turbulent divorce. Consequently, Lucy gained control of the majority voting shares, while Adityan was unceremoniously expelled from the company with nothing to show for his time there.

The audiobook came to a sudden pause as the car's screen showed an incoming call. A smiling picture of Paul with his beautiful light brown eyes appeared. Lucy pressed the accept button.

'What is it, Paul? How many times do I have to tell you not to disturb me in the early morning hours?'

'Just wanted to check if our evening date is still on. I've booked a table for us at Le Cirque. You mentioned you wanted to try more Italian cuisine, so I called the sous chef, who's also my …'

'Paul, didn't I tell you last time to call my assistant? Sara handles all my appointments. And if I'm free, we can meet.'

'All right, Lucy. That's perfect! I'll be sitting with my father at the investor meeting. Remember to greet him with respect— you know how the oldies are.'

'I need to end the call now, I'm driving,' said Lucy and she ended the call.

Somehow, the conversation stirred a raw nerve deep within Lucy. Her hands trembled as she opened the car's dashboard, searching frantically for the one thing that would relieve her stress—the small bottles of Jack Daniel's she kept hidden in the car for emergencies. As her fingers closed around one, her breath hitched and pressure mounted in her chest. She uncapped the bottle and, with a shaky hand, gulped down its contents in a single, burning swallow.

Paul is a good man—tall, handsome and from a well-respected family. He clearly likes me. But do I like him? Is he going to be just another Adityan, someone who will worm his way into my lonely life only to leave me shattered and broken?

Adityan's face materialised in her mind—not the furious expression she last saw when security escorted him from the office, but the tender visage she cherished from their earlier days. *How is he doing? Does he still care about me? Do I still miss him?*

With these thoughts swirling in her mind, Lucy reached her office and parked the car. She checked her hair and make-up and made sure she was presentable, before smoothly getting out of her vehicle and walking to the building. Outside the glass door stood a man in a blue security uniform. 'Good morning, madam', he said while saluting her.

24

'So, what was last quarter's profit?'

'₹18 crore.'

'Hmm. Can you tell me more about the revenue and expenses for the quarter?'

'Sure,' Lucy cleared her throat. 'Our revenue was ₹70 crore, with expenses of ₹52 crore, leading to the aforementioned profit. Of the expenses, ₹10 crore was spent on expanding our operations in new markets, ₹15 crore on research and development and ₹27 crore was spent on general and administrative expenses.'

'What about the growth rate compared to the previous quarter and the same quarter last year?'

'Right now, we're in a phase of hypergrowth.' Lucy pointed to the presentation slide that was projected on the screen. 'Ten per cent compared to the previous quarter is just the tip of the iceberg. We've outperformed the market with a growth rate of 50 per cent compared to the same quarter of the previous year. It's not your usual run-of-the-mill kind of growth, it's something special.'

'Impressive, right?' Paul looked at his father and his advisers, who were trying hard to find faults with Lucy's presentation.

'How much do you expect us to invest?'

'We're looking to raise ₹100 crore to continue our expansion into new markets and further invest in research and development to maintain our position as the market leader in this industry.'

The men in suits exchanged glances, the phrase '₹100 crore' lingering in the room like a guest who had overstayed her welcome. There was a palpable pause before Jacob Fernandes, Paul's father, finally broke the silence. 'And in return for this investment,' he asked, 'what kind of equity are you proposing to offer?'

'We're offering a 20 per cent stake in the company in return; the number of board seats is negotiable.'

'What about your ex-husband, the co-founder? What was his name?' Fernandes tapped his finger over the table '… Adityan Roy.'

'What about him?'

'Doesn't he still own a portion of the voting shares? We can't take any sort of risk when it comes to our investments. A rogue co-founder is always an unwanted crapshoot.'

'Adityan is under control, my lawyers have already taken care of him. We will reach a settlement with him prior to finalising our deal. After that he will no longer be a shareholder in the company and won't have a say in decision-making.' Lucy paused for a moment before continuing in a passive tone, 'And if he tries something funny, I will personally make sure to burn him to the ground.'

'We'll still have to conduct our final assessments and evaluations, of course. I'll despatch my team for that. Otherwise, let's consider this a done deal. Shall we seal it with a gentleman's handshake?' A smile appeared on Jacob Fernandes's face as he stood up and extended his hand towards Lucy. She instantly grabbed it and shook it tightly.

She had a deal—that too on her terms. Lucy felt satisfied and happy. But as soon as the man withdrew his hand and turned to face his colleagues, a feeling of emptiness overtook her heart. She had imagined that this accomplishment would amount to something significant. Yet now that it was within her grasp, the pointlessness of it all was painfully evident.

'Congratulations, Lucy, that was smooth.' It was Paul tapping her shoulder. 'Don't forget our evening plan,' he whispered gently in her ear.

As the celebratory pop of the champagne bottle echoed from the conference room, Lucy quietly slipped away to the sanctuary of the restroom. There she started weeping like a child who had got lost in a crowded arena. Through watery eyes, she scrolled through photos of Adityan, Zacharia and her family on her phone.

By the time she returned, the celebrations had moved from the meeting room to the main office. More of her colleagues from the marketing, IT and research departments had gathered in the large hall.

'Lucy, the boss lady, she's pulled it off again!' she heard someone in the crowd say. A toast followed. Lucy's lips curved upwards, but her eyes told a different story.

25

'What am I doing with my life?'

A tall and well-groomed man dressed in a crisp white shirt, black pants and tie walked towards the candlelit table where the special guests were seated. In his hand was a silver platter that he carried with confidence.

The fine dining restaurant maintained its characteristic hushed ambiance, with soft jazz playing in the background. The young man set the platter down in front of his guests and, with a flourish, lifted the cover to unveil the special meal garnished with herbs and edible flowers.

'Madam, sir, this is Lobster Thermidor, our main course for the day. This dish is a true delicacy, featuring a whole lobster expertly shelled and cut into succulent pieces. The lobster is then combined with a creamy sauce made from a blend of butter, shallots, white wine and mustard, giving it a rich and luxurious flavour. Topped with grated cheese and baked to perfection, it is both decadent and delicious.' The man looked at both his guests to make sure they were listening before continuing. 'I would recommend a very special wine to accompany your meal tonight, the Château Margaux. This wine is a true masterpiece, produced in the Bordeaux region of France from a blend of the finest Cabernet Sauvignon, Merlot, Cabernet Franc and Petit Verdot grapes. An elegant and complex flavour profile, featuring notes of black cherry, plum, cassis and vanilla. Shall I pour a glass for you?'

'Yes, please.' Lucy pushed her glass towards him. The man bowed before pouring the wine into her glass. Before he could explain how to drink it the right way, Lucy gulped it down and asked him to pour some more. Paul smiled confidently and gestured the waiter to keep the bottle on the table.

'So, Lucy, you didn't answer my last question,' Paul asked after the waiter departed.

'Did you ask me something?' she inquired, her tongue struggling to articulate the words clearly.

'Yes. I've heard rumours that you aren't the easiest of people to deal with. Is that true?'

'What does that mean?'

'Well, that you are a blunt person. We have been meeting on and off for almost three months and not even once have you invited me to your place.'

'And why should I do that?' Lucy placed a hand on her forehead, feeling dizzy from the alcohol coursing through her veins.

'We are both adults, and we all have our needs. We don't have to play these mind games.' Paul's voice carried a hint of provocation. 'If you are not thinking about calling me home, I'd like to invite myself. Or even better, why not come to my place later?'

'What are you talking about, Paul? Don't be like those idiots in Tinder, always looking for excuses to sleep with a girl. Grow up!' Lucy mocked him.

'I have a feeling that you used me to get to my father, and I am not fond of manipulation. Why else are you keeping your distance? Look at me, I am a perfectly fine gentleman,' he replied in a rigid tone.

'Can you please open that window? It's getting stuffy in here; I can hardly breathe!' Lucy ignored Paul's comment and rose to her feet and started shouting at the waiter. The abruptness of her outcry tore through the tranquil atmosphere, like a stone cast into a still pond. The other guests looked at them curiously as the waiter hastily flung the window open.

'What are you doing, Lucy? Please behave.'

'I'm not sure what you're after, Paul, but you won't find it here, not with me,' she sighed. 'It's been an exhausting day. Perhaps we should wrap things up after dinner.'

Paul's face fell, his hopes dashed. He brooded briefly before offering a new proposal. 'You might want to seriously think about not driving tonight. Let me drive you home.'

'Maybe, maybe,' Lucy mumbled, as the bitter taste of half-digested food filled her mouth. The urge to vomit was overwhelming now. She sprang from her chair and sprinted to the bathroom. 'Are you okay?' She heard Paul's concern from behind her, but there was no time to reply.

The moment she entered the women's bathroom she threw up straight into the sparkling clean sink. A portion of it made its way to the towels placed beside it. She glanced up at the gleaming mirror and stared into her bloodshot eyes. *What was I thinking?*

Lucy's fingers curled around the brass tap, and a surge of ice-cold water rushed forth. Gathering a palmful, she gently washed her face, her eyes closed as if in silent prayer. In the heart of that invigorating sensation, a soft whisper touched her soul. 'Lucy … tread carefully.' The words faded like mist, leaving behind a vision that blossomed within her.

Meanwhile, Paul was busy at the table. He reached into his pocket to retrieve a pill. With practised ease, he crushed it between his fingers, the powder almost invisible against his pale skin. He discreetly mixed the powder into a glass of water before sliding it next to Lucy's plate. 'I thought all that alcohol would do the trick … Let's see how you handle a dose of Zolpidem,' he muttered under his breath. The white powder dissolved in the water, leaving only a faint memory of its presence.

Startled by the vision, Lucy immediately opened her eyes. The tap continued to run, its rhythmic gushing filling her ears. *What was all that? Am I dozing off?* After taking a few steady breaths, she returned to the table. From the distance, Lucy could see a seemingly innocent glass of water waiting for her.

26

With a click of the small button, the car roof retracted, revealing the cacophony of city life—blaring horns, bustling crowds and distant tunes blending with the pop music inside the car.

Lucy raised her hands, embracing the exhilarating rush of cool breeze that soft droplets of rain had brought with it. Almost instinctively, she unbuckled her seatbelt and rose from her seat. Her hair whipped behind her while her blue shirt danced in the breeze like a billowing kite.

'What are you doing, Lucy? Sit down. It's not safe,' Paul warned, keeping his eyes on the road.

'My car, my rules. Your chauffeur duties don't give you the right to boss me around. Just zip it and drive,' she retorted playfully.

'Please, Lucy, sit down. We are almost there,' Paul urged, steering the car away from the main road and into the eerily quiet and isolated service roads that seemed to diverge from the familiar urban landscape.

'Are we almost there? This doesn't look like my street. How do you plan to get home after dropping me off? You could always borrow this car and return it in the morning. I won't mind,' she slurred, her words weighed down by the disorienting haze enveloping her.

'We will have a quick stop at another place before I drop you.'

'What place? Why?'

'Why not?' Paul said as he turned left. A sprawling, secluded villa gradually came into view. The gates sensed the approaching vehicle and swung open without delay. He navigated the car into the underground parking space.

'We are almost home. Just hang in tight.' Paul parked the car next to the other vehicles, and briskly guided Lucy by the shoulder towards the elevator, disregarding her persistent objections.

Inside the villa, he quickly seated her on the sofa, then darted to the bedroom to close all the windows and align the pillows.

Meanwhile, Lucy teetered on the edge of consciousness, utterly drained. Her lips were parched and her mouth felt dry. All she craved was the solace of her own bed and the chance to shut her eyes. As the minutes ticked by, she succumbed to the inviting embrace of the sofa and drifted into an unbidden slumber. Her mind gently tiptoed into the uncharted territory of dreams.

Lucy suddenly found herself standing on a rugged, rocky floor. In front of her, perched on a magnificent throne, sat a man with three distinct faces holding a crystal ball. His first countenance mirrored a formidable bull, its snout sharp and daunting. The second resembled a snake, hissing with malevolence. The third face, however, was that of a man—a man whose face stirred a faint memory in her mind. She struggled to remember where she had encountered him before.

The humanoid creature appeared to be deeply troubled, as if he was acutely aware of an imminent misfortune.

'Lucy … Lucy … You are in danger. Wake up and get out of there,' it cried, staring into the crystal ball.

'What?' she replied. 'Are you talking to me?'

'There is no time to explain. You must leave from there, right now.' The warning continued, 'Danger, danger, danger.' His grip on the crystal ball tightened as it started to shudder, glowing like a star nearing explosion. Its brightness blinded Lucy. She closed her eyes, falling into another vision.

Paul donned a white sleeveless vest and loose-fitting trousers, the belt buckle deliberately left partially undone. He crept towards the room, cautiously observing from a distance to ensure the woman he had brought home was indeed asleep.

With calculated precision, he quietly approached Lucy and lifted her in his arms. Much like a predator brining its prey to its lair, he took her to his dimly lit room and laid her on the bed.

Paul began to undress her while humming a melody to himself. Lucy attempted to rise twice, but her drunkenness held her down, leaving her vulnerable to his advances. After removing his own clothes, Paul approached her, his intent clear as he gradually slid her pants off. With a sinister smirk, he taunted, 'What now? Where's the boss lady now?'

The vision ended, and Lucy bounced up from the sofa and turned around. In the distance, she could see the man looking at her like a wild animal. He had taken off his shirt and his pants were on the floor.

'Are you all right?' He walked towards her as if nothing strange had happened.

Lucy felt like her legs had frozen. Every nerve had shut down in response to the overwhelming fear. *What do I do now?* Her heart pounded and adrenaline coursed through her veins as the spark of survival instinct ignited within her. Her eyes moved around the room, rapidly piecing together an escape plan.

In the distance, she spotted her car keys. The door was close by too. Scattered on the floor around it was Paul's workout equipment. Like a seasoned acrobat, she rolled over on the sofa to the other side of the room. Along the way, she snatched the car keys from the table and sprinted towards the door. She pulled the handle, but it was locked.

'Where do you think you are going? No one is going anywhere tonight,' Paul said, moving closer towards Lucy, showing the key he held in his hand.

'Paul, this is not funny, and I am not going to give you another warning. Let me go right now … or …' Lucy screamed while continuing her efforts to open the door.

'Or what? You will sue—' His words were cut short as Lucy sprang into action. She quickly grabbed a dumbbell from the floor and struck him on the head. The force of the first blow took Paul by surprise. He fell to the floor and blood seeped from his forehead. The second strike landed on his left cheek, splattering blood across her clothes. After the third blow, he lay motionless on the floor. Without missing a beat, Lucy snatched the key from his hand and sprinted back to the door. Flinging it open, she hurried down the corridor in search of an exit. Spotting a staircase, she descended to the underground parking area.

27

The car raced along the rain-slicked streets of Bannerghatta, its tyres struggling to maintain traction amidst the torrential monsoon downpour. Drains overflowed and a thick fog settled in, shrouding the late night in a mysterious veil.

Lucy's heart pounded as she fought to focus, her hands quivering from the aftershock of what had just happened. She glanced at her clothes that were stained with blood. She couldn't help but wonder if Paul had died.

On the infotainment system on the car, the call she had placed to Uncle George was going unanswered. Before reaching out to him, Lucy had attempted to contact Jessy, her trusted personal assistant, and then Pratap Reddy, the commissioner of police. But at 2.00 a.m., it seemed as if the entire world was sleeping.

The call rang for what felt like an eternity before abruptly giving way to a prerecorded voice message. A shiver ran down Lucy's spine as she fumbled with the dashboard, searching for any remaining PET bottles of alcohol.

Her fingertips brushed against one, and she quickly snatched it, bringing it to her lips for a desperate sip.

A fleeting sense of calmness washed over her as the alcohol did its job. But that moment of tranquillity stirred a haunting murmur, a voice gently cautioning her once again: 'You've been changing, gradually losing sight of the person you once were. It seems as though the distance between us only widens with time. Have you forgotten my presence?'

A wave of enlightenment coursed through her being, revitalising her senses. A flash of lightning in the sky illuminated a towering roadside billboard. It showcased a radiant golden lamp nestled within the outstretched palms of a djinn. She saw his green eyes locked on a woman engrossed in her phone. Bold text soared above the scene: 'Unlock a World of Magic with DjinnDaddy. Make a wish, now!'

Unbeknownst to her, the image triggered a torrent of memories. Memories of Zacharia's death, the funeral, the lamp, the djinn and her wish to alter the future all flooded back like a tsunami, consuming everything in its path and leaving only confusion and bewilderment in its wake. *Iblis,* she wondered, *is it you who warned me?*

Uncle George's name flashed on the car's screen. Lucy looked away from the road to answer the call. At the same time, a truck emerged from the crossroad four hundred metres ahead of her. Its exhausted driver fought to keep his eyes open. The truck's engine roared as he accelerated, rapidly approaching a sharp, blind turn.

Just before completing the curve, he collided with Lucy's car at breakneck speed. The truck spiralled out of control, wheeling sharply to the left and smashing into a rock wall. Meanwhile, Lucy's car careened to the right, shattering the safety barrier and flinging through the air before plunging into the depths of the lake that abutted the road.

28

When Lucy woke up, she was standing in an unnervingly infinite expanse of white. The silence was punctuated only by the static hum of a machine, sending a frisson of unease rippling through her. Disoriented and unsure of how she had arrived here, she squinted to make out a distant shape. The outline of a blue sofa and a television emerged from the white abyss. The screen flickered with a dance of black-and-white dots, indicating a lost signal.

'Helloooo, anyone here?' Lucy asked nervously as she navigated towards the oasis in the sea of white, finally settling onto a divan.

The screen before her continued to flicker erratically, the static sound growing louder. In the next split, a video sprang to life. She saw a towering, human-like figure sitting regally on an opulent throne and cradling an enormous crystal ball in its grasp. Unwavering, he gazed into the shimmering orb.

Where am I? Lucy moved closer to the television. The brightness increased. She could see the figure better now, it's sad face and glowing green eyes that stared at the unknown.

'Iblis,' Lucy whispered, her voice barely audible to herself. She stretched out her trembling fingers, making contact with the cool, flat surface. To her astonishment, her hands penetrated the screen. With a mix of curiosity and trepidation, she pushed herself forward and disappeared into the enigmatic realm beyond.

Upon stepping into this otherworldly space, Lucy was immediately engulfed by a feeling of chilling darkness and desolation. Around her was a harsh and unforgiving terrain marred by jagged rocks and fractured stones.

Within the cracks of the scorched earth, molten fluids simmered and the sky above was cloaked in impenetrable blackness, devoid of stars, as if under the spell of an eternal eclipse. Amidst this landscape, Iblis sat on a throne, his unyielding gaze fixed upon the enchanting sphere in his grasp.

'Iblis, where am I?' Lucy inquired.

The imposing figure remained motionless, seemingly oblivious to her presence.

'Can you hear me, Iblis? Answer me!' she demanded, her voice rising in frustration.

Confused by his lack of reaction, Lucy walked towards the djinn. As she moved closer, Lucy saw a three-dimensional image of a woman materialising within the depths of the crystal. She was young and elegantly dressed, and sleeping peacefully in her bed.

When will you wake up, my dear Olga? Lucy's heart was suddenly touched by a whisper. She felt a wave of emotions. The sensation was delicate, almost imperceptible at first, but soon it grew in intensity, enveloping her in a shroud of feelings.

Olga? she asked herself. *Who's that?*

In endless wait, I yearned for thee, the one whose heart beats true and free, with you, my soul finds its abode, you are the key, my freedom's code. Iblis's thoughts continued to surge through her, battering her consciousness like a tempestuous sea. Lucy struggled against its tides as they pulled her deeper into the abyss. She tried to hold on to herself, to find some anchor to cling to, but everything was slipping away from her grasp. Without even realising it, Lucy became part of the djinn's thoughts. She merged with them and sailed through the waves of his past.

29

'Ah, it is I who whispers in your dreams.'

After the death of Alexander the Great, his vast empire
fragmented into smaller territories, each governed by one of

his battle-hardened generals. These skilled tacticians, known collectively as the Diadochi, divided the spoils of his conquests among themselves, claiming the riches that had once belonged to the king they had served.

Among these riches was the magical lamp that was taken to the Royal Treasury.

Once again, the djinn was trapped inside with no option but to return to his silent meditation. He went back to his memories, placing himself on a ghostly throne inside the lamp, watching the world from its dimly lit vantage point.

Having lost faith in humans, he took a vow of silence and swore off any further interaction with humankind.

Another two hundred years passed.

The next major conflict to impact Babylon occurred in the second century BCE when the Seleucid king Antiochus III the Great invaded and ransacked the city. As part of the spoils of war, the lamp was taken along with other treasures, finding its way to Antiochus III's capital, Antioch.

The djinn's silent vigil continued even as he witnessed the constant changes in the world's landscape.

In the decades that followed, the lamp was passed through the hands of several Seleucid rulers, including Antiochus IV Epiphanes and Demetrius I Soter, until it was ultimately taken by the Romans during the conquest of Syria. The lamp was then taken to Rome, where it was stored in the Imperial Palace and displayed as a symbol of victory.

As the centuries rolled on, the lamp vanished from the annals of history, only to resurface in the sixth century, cradled in the hands of Byzantine Emperor Justinian I. It was gifted to him by a war general, Belisarius, who led a campaign in Italy in the mid-sixth century CE and looted several major cities, including Ravenna and Rome.

After Justinian's death, the lamp was moved to the Hagia Sophia in Constantinople until it was stolen during the Fourth Crusade in 1204. It was then smuggled to Venice, where it remained in the possession of wealthy families.

In the waning years of the nineteenth century, a Russian art collector acquired the lamp, transporting it to Moscow. There, it graced the halls of various museums and art fairs, captivating onlookers as an Egyptian relic.

Two decades from then, a woman named Olga stumbled upon the lamp at an auction, purchasing it as a gift for her beloved husband, Nikolai, an aspiring artist. The moment Olga's fingers brushed against the lamp, Iblis stirred from his solemn silence. Her touch roused him from his self-imposed exile.

On the very night that Olga welcomed the lamp into her home, the djinn slipped into her dreams and leafed through the pages of her memories.

Born in Nizhyn, Ukraine, Olga Kholova was the daughter of Russian Imperial Army Colonel Ivan Khokhlov and his wife, Lyubov Beloborodova. Fuelled by an unwavering passion for dance, Olga soared to the esteemed ranks of Bolshoi Ballet after graduating from the renowned Mikhailovsky Art School.

Her path crossed Nikolai's when she saw him designing sets and costumes for the Ballets Russes production of *Parade*. From the moment their eyes met, they were captivated by one another.

The djinn watched as Olga and Nikolai exchanged vows in Moscow and began a life together. He bore witness to her pain and passion, and how she set aside her ambitions to nurture their love.

Among the countless humans he had encountered—fraught with cowardice and treachery—Olga stood apart. She was the solitary golden flower in a world riddled with deceit. Iblis found himself increasingly drawn to her, captivated by her pure thoughts. He longed to claim her as his own.

A week after the lamp's arrival in her home, Olga started hearing mysterious whispers. They told her that her husband was having an affair with a seventeen-year-old girl named Marie-Therese. The whispers also urged her to open the lamp, promising that she would meet an ancient orator who could reveal more about Nikolai's secrets.

Although the strange experience frightened Olga, the thought of her beloved husband being unfaithful was unbearable. Once she had steadied her nerves, she carefully opened the ancient artefact.

A dense green fog emerged from the lamp, catching Olga off guard. Startled, she dropped the lamp and fled to her bedroom, quickly locking the door and propping a chair against it. Not long after, a knock sounded, followed by a male voice speaking broken Russian, 'Olga, why are you afraid? I'm here to help.'

'What kind of demon are you?'

'I am no demon,' the male voice replied calmly. 'Think of me as the Koschei, Domovoi or the Vodyanoy that your grandmother used to tell you about in childhood stories. I am the one from fairy tales. I have been sent to protect you. And in return, you can grant me freedom.'

'How do you know what my grandmother used to tell me?'

'Oh, Olga, I know you better than you know yourself. I've seen your memories unfold, your dreams and your fears left untold. I have seen your love, a story yet to be told. You're dear to me, that much is true. For in this world, there's none like you.' The djinn sang in a melodious voice, leaving Olga with the feeling that she was hearing the divine harmony of an angel. 'Open the door, and make a wish. I'll reveal all that you want to know.'

Upon opening the door, she was greeted by a man who bore a striking resemblance to her first love in Nizhyn. Tall and broad-shouldered, he had thick eyebrows and piercing green eyes. He tenderly took her hand and led her to sit on a wooden chair in the stairway.

'Consider me a humble servant who was destined to meet you at this moment. I'll grant you three wishes; use them wisely. Make each one meaningful and grand. Once they're fulfilled, I'll take my leave.'

As expected, Olga's first wish was to see the true desires of her husband's heart. Iblis revealed to her all of Nikolai's actions and the thoughts that led to them.

She witnessed his affairs, his mistresses and his deceit. She learnt about his lust for others. Olga felt desperate and broken. She cried loudly, condemning everything about herself. But not once did she blame her husband for his wrongdoings. This surprised Iblis.

'Why do you still blame yourself, Olga? Why bear the burden of another's wrongs?' he asked.

'Oh, Koschei. Don't you already know?' she cried. 'Love is a promise we make, to stand by each other, come what may. Love isn't easy, it's true. It takes sacrifice and courage. Sometimes we take the blame for the sake of love. It is how we heal our hearts, both mine and his ...' Olga sang. Her feet began to move of their own accord. It was a dance of pain.

30

In a universe where the concepts of right and wrong were nebulous, what set people apart was the purity of their hearts, intentions and actions. The djinn, with his immense wisdom and eons-long existence, was already aware of this. After he started living with Olga, as her invisible Koschei, love blossomed in his heart. He started gifting her things without being asked, but Olga refused to accept them.

Despite her husband's constant betrayal and deceit, Olga continued to pray for his health and well-being. Kneeling before sacred statues, she begged the gods to lead him back to her.

'Oh, Olga, my dear, why keep yourself in the shadows? What do you hope to gain, apart from silent pain? Don't you dream of a life of grandeur, to be a princess in a far-off land, with me as your guardian and beau.' Iblis constantly tried to lure her towards him, surprised by the resilience of her affection for a man who didn't care for her.

'I am a servant of love, this is my path, to care for those I love until my last breath. Without them, I am but a lost soul,' she would always reply. And as her words drifted through the air, they imbued the djinn with an overwhelming sensation of tenderness. The intensity of this feelings left him spellbound.

But Olga's kindness wasn't just for the man she had married, it extended to the djinn too. She often expressed her gratitude to Iblis for coming into her life as a messenger. But she would always gently inform him that his guidance was no longer required.

Her desire, she explained, was to journey on the path the gods had etched for her and then meet her end. She believed she lacked nothing in life except the love of the man who held a place in her heart. She was sure he would find his way to her in due course.

Eventually, the djinn stopped urging her to seek wealth and fame, or tricking her into falling in love with him, and allowed her to call upon him only in times of dire need. He retreated to the solitude of his lamp, patiently waiting for another wish to be made.

Ten years later, Olga's second wish came to pass. She lay ill with tuberculosis in the sterile silence of a hospital room. Her once vibrant skin was now a pallid, sweat-dampened shell. Her lively eyes had faded into tired, sunken hollows. The spectre of death, uninvited yet persistent, drew its shadowy cloak tighter around her.

'Koschei, if you are around and watching me, I need help,' she cried.

In that very moment, Iblis appeared with open arms. 'What does your heart seek, my dear Olga?' he asked.

'Save me from this sickness, save me from this pain. Don't let me die,' she pleaded.

Iblis took a deep breath and held it briefly before blowing it over her face. Olga's body jolted as if electrified. Her eyes cleared and her skin regained its glow. She rose from her deathbed and hopped onto the floor. Like a newborn, she felt omnipotent. Olga fell to her knees and started weeping.

As soon as she was discharged from the hospital, Olga rushed home, wondering why her beloved husband hadn't been visiting lately. His absence made her angry and sad.

But what awaited her at home was the heart-wrenching sight of her husband lying lifeless on the floor. Assuming his wife would not survive, Nikolai took his own life. He had mixed potassium cyanide into his nightly drink and chose to meet death on his own terms.

Olga was devastated.

She summoned the djinn once again, begging him to breathe life back into her deceased husband. But Iblis lowered his head and told her that resurrection was beyond his capabilities. Once a soul had journeyed beyond the veil of life, there was no path that led back. He gently revealed that upon entering the otherworld, a soul is faced with a choice—to reincarnate or to become one with the cosmos. Nikolai had chosen the latter.

'Olga, even the divine gods cannot reverse death's cold decree. His time had come, and he has journeyed to where his spirit belongs. If he had chosen rebirth's call, I would have led you to his birthplace. But Nikolai chose to disperse, to go with the stars.'

'If he's ventured beyond mortal shores, then I too will seek that. For love, I'll chase each distant star,' Olga said and took a gulp from the half-empty bottle that lay beside her husband's body.

'Don't … don't!' Iblis screamed in great anguish. But Olga was determined to end her life. Iblis could do nothing about it.

The moment her soul departed her body, Iblis swiftly caught it with his magic and trapped it in his lamp. In retribution for granting an unspoken wish, the lamp claimed the djinn's left eye. It left him with excruciating pain.

However, despite his efforts, Iblis couldn't retain Olga's soul for long. When the call of fate reached her ears, Olga faced a choice—rebirth or merge into the whole.

'Come and find me,' she said, before disappearing from his memories, choosing to be born again, almost hundred years later as Zacharia Cheriyan's first grandchild.

31

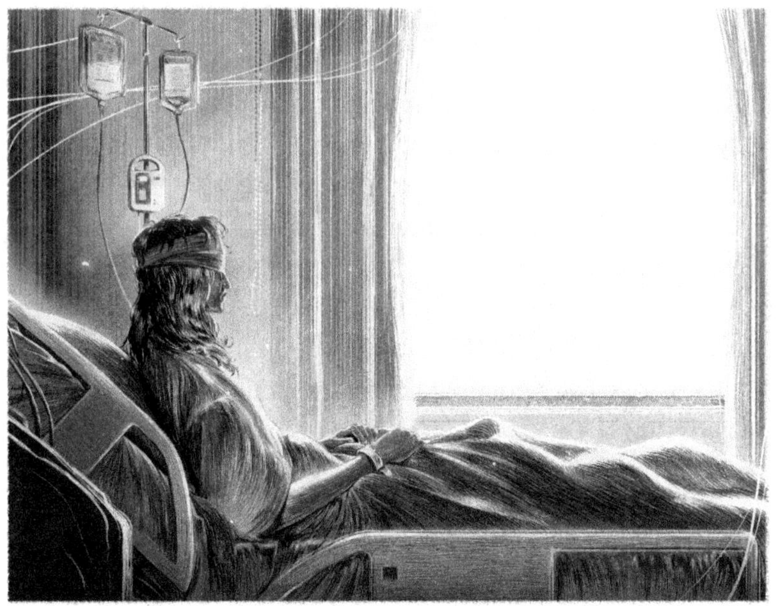

'Praise the lord ... Praise the lord'

Lucy woke up in a hospital bed with an oxygen tube in her nose. She glanced at the wires attached to her chest and the IV line on the back of her hand. She felt as though her body had been crushed into pieces and reassembled.

Visions of the car crash returned with striking clarity. Her car somersaulting into the lake, the sudden impact causing the airbags to inflate, her face and arms smashing into one, the sound of the windshield breaking, the water creeping into the car.

She recollected how she desperately tried to open the doors as blood oozed through her broken nose and how the lake pulled her deeper into its grasp. Lucy felt a cold shiver over her skin.

What happened then? A name came to her mind, that of the djinn. In her desperation, she had summoned him. As she was slowing sinking into the lake, she saw a fire above the lake. Out of that came a creature, the bull, the snake, the man—Iblis.

'Are you awake?' Lucy heard Jancy chechi's voice. It sounded muffled as if she was still submerged under water. 'Lucy molae, are you awake?'

'Doctor, doctor, she is awake!' Jancy chechi screamed as she dashed from the room, seeking assistance.

How long have I been out? Lucy tried to lift herself off the bed, but searing pain shot through her jaw, hip and left leg. 'Aaaaa!' A cry escaped her lips as the reality of her injuries set in. Swathed in white bandages, she couldn't discern which wounds they masked. The yellow and red stains suggested some were recent, perhaps only days old. Confused and scared, Lucy continued her struggle to get off the bed.

'Lucy, please remain still,' instructed the man in the doctor's coat who swiftly entered the room. 'How are you feeling? It's completely normal to experience disorientation and confusion after waking up from a coma. Please don't be alarmed.'

'How long have I been here? How did I get—'

'Pulse seems to be fine,' the doctor said as he pressed on her wrist.

'How long have I been here?' Lucy raised her voice.

'Eighteen days.' He scribbled something in his notepad. 'Relax,' he murmured gently.

'And how did I get here?' Lucy was getting restless.

When the doctor didn't reply, she decided to protest, leaning on the simple legal principles every person knew. 'As my doctor, you are obligated to answer my questions. Answer me. Now.'

'When they brought you here, you did not have a pulse. There were no vital signs of life. The emergency doctor confirmed your death. But then while they were moving you to the mortuary, one of the attendees saw your fingers twitching.' The doctor looked at the EEG machine and took the reading. 'You were underwater for twelve minutes, I know no one who has ever survived that. You are a medical miracle.'

'Praise the Lord … Praise the Lord. Let me call George and the others,' Jancy chechi started weeping.

32

The next three months flew past with dizzying haste. After her discharge, Lucy found herself back in her apartment. The familiar surroundings—her hardwood kitchen floor, the drooping foliage of her plants and the ceaseless chatter of her Google devices—served as a brief salve to her weary spirit.

However, under the veneer of mending ribs and a slowly healing collarbone, she could feel her life unravelling at an alarming pace. In her enforced absence, Adityan had skilfully wielded his influence, orchestrating a coup that resulted in her abrupt and ungracious removal from the CEO's position.

To make matters worse, the investment she'd worked so hard to secure had inexplicably gone awry. Although Paul had refrained from pressing charges, he paid her a chilling visit in the hospital. When he told her that she'd never build another successful company again, she couldn't stop shivering for a few minutes.

As if that wasn't enough, the media had caught wind of her drunk driving incident. With her reputation in tatters, she had to face the humiliation of standing in court and offering a public apology for jeopardising the safety of others. Her spirit had been truly bruised and battered, leaving her wondering if there was any way to rise from the ashes.

A few days ago, the minute Jancy chechi had entered the apartment, she embarked on a methodical exploration of every cabinet. She tactfully drained any alcohol she found into the sink and discarded the empty bottles. Lucy, her spirit muted and her mind lost in thought, raised no objections to the purge.

Lounging on her couch, Lucy found herself thinking about the past. She revisited her youth, the hurdles she had faced after her parents' death and the enduring affection bestowed upon her by her grandparents, Zacharia and Susanna.

Adityan and Paul too crept into her musings, initially igniting a flame of resentment—*such despicable men*, she seethed. But as time passed, she unearthed a well of forgiveness, releasing them from her emotional grip. Tender memories of her husband surfaced—their shared love, laughter and support. She felt guilty for judging him harshly, despite empathising with his troubled upbringing.

Overcome with the urge to make amends, Lucy took her phone and sent Adityan a sincere message: 'I've been hard on you for years, and I'm truly sorry. Our difficult pasts played a role, but that's no excuse. I hope you can find it in your heart to forgive me and cherish the good times we had. Wishing you the best, always.'

She waited and waited, but no reply came.

Maybe he thinks it is just another of my schemes to regain control of the company, Lucy thought as she ruminated about her tendency to be impulsive.

Her forgiveness didn't extend to Paul. She chastised herself for being careless, recalling the numerous times she had deliberately sent him mixed signals to get a leg up in the cut-throat start-up world. Shame washed over her as she realised she had become the very person she despised: someone who exploits others' vulnerabilities for personal gain. *How could I judge others when we're all fragile beings striving to exist?*

As Lucy found some semblance of peace, her thoughts wandered to Iblis. At first, she had been uncertain about the stranger who had appeared in her life. Yet, as the initial shock wore off, a profound and ineffable bond emerged between them. A connection so deep and intense that she often denied its existence.

In Iblis's absence, she felt an inexplicable void, as if a fragment of herself had been excised, leaving her heart yearning for his presence.

Where are you, my djinn? Why do you continue to elude me? I've made peace with my past and forgiven all that can be forgiven. I've abandoned my vices, relinquished my prejudices and sought redemption. Why can't I hear your voice? Why won't you answer my calls? She longed for his comforting presence and the feeling of completeness that he brought into her life.

But despite her earnest pleas and the heartfelt desire that gripped her soul, Iblis remained silent. And Lucy was left to wrestle with a haunting question—would she ever hear from him again?

33

By the end of the year, Lucy had decided to sell her shares in Picasso and rent out her apartment.

She had spent so much of her youth sculpting her business from an idea that it had become her life's purpose. But as she maintained her distance from alcohol, she began to question the true value of material wealth, social status and the allure of success as seen by others. Her introspection led her to examine the path she had chosen and the person she had become. She couldn't help but wonder why she had decided to develop a mobile app instead of embracing her love for painting, and how that had caused her to leave her grandparents behind.

And then one day, as though the universe had been eavesdropping on her thoughts, a sign materialised. It occurred on one of those afternoons when she and Jancy chechi watched an old Malayalam classic. The protagonist of the film—a wealthy businessman—found himself grappling with the hollow resonance of his materialistic pursuits and made the profound decision to shed the weight of his possessions and adopt the life of a hermit.

Before leaving his home, he turned to his wife and delivered a heartfelt dialogue: 'There used to be a man in my heart who was free from desire and despair, who did not succumb to the temptations of the world. I thought he was just a dreamer, a misguided soul who believed he had life all figured out. So, I neglected him and gave way to the other who always searched for a thousand praises. But now, life has shown me the truth, urging me to let go of all I've built in search of the man I once was.'

Lucy, for a fleeting moment, felt as though the man on the screen was speaking directly to her. At first, it made her smile. *What a joke!* she thought, but then the idea slowly took root within her, growing and expanding like a plant seed reaching for the surface.

It took her back to the verdant garden at Palathikal House with its blossoming flowers and melodious birdsong that rang throughout the day.

She remembered the carefree afternoons spent sipping tea with Susanna, unburdened by the weight of tomorrow's concerns. Those thoughts stirred a deep sense of nostalgia in Lucy. She longed for the simplicity of those bygone days. She envisioned what it might be like to return to her ancestral home, to leave behind all that weighed her down and sleep in her childhood bed—if it remained.

Lucy turned to Jancy chechi and asked about the current state of her beloved home. She learnt that after Zacharia's passing, their ancestral home had briefly been in Jancy chechi's possession, as per her grandfather's will. However, societal pressures had compelled her to relinquish the property to Elza, his youngest daughter. The house was now rented out to a family whose identity she didn't know.

In a flurry of determination, Lucy made multiple calls to the USA, attempting to get in touch with her aunt and negotiate with her husband to buy back the ancestral home. It was Lucy's offer to pay double the estimated cost for the house and the estate that ultimately convinced them.

When the agreement was signed and finalised, Lucy gifted the old tharavadu back to Jancy chechi, her aged caretaker, as a token of appreciation for her unwavering support in times of need.

Upon returning to the Palathikal estate, Lucy got in touch with a local animal shelter to adopt a puppy. She named him Tipu and made a solemn promise never to restrain him with a leash.

The recently erected asbestos shed at the back of the mansion was taken apart, and, in its place, Lucy envisioned the restoration of the once enchanting garden that had thrived there. Fragrant jasmine and marigold blossoms intertwining with the vibrant magenta of bougainvillea, while coconut and mango trees provided shade. Meandering stone pathways, inlaid with traditional Athangudi tiles, would lead guests through the lush landscape, where they would encounter a lotus-filled pond and the soothing sound of fountains.

Lucy also contemplated an elegant transformation of the interiors—a delicate interplay of ochre, indigo and warm earth tones enveloping the walls while aged teakwood floors, polished to mirror-like perfection, gleaming underfoot.

Embracing each emotion and memory, Lucy meticulously infused every cherished detail from her childhood into the place, quickly transforming it into her haven. And as she immersed herself into the making of the home, long-lost habits seamlessly returned, making her feel more connected to the world around her.

She acquired a portable easel, paintbrushes, a palette and acrylic colours, and set up a workshop facing the setting sun.

At first, her fingers felt awkward and hesitant as they made contact with the paint. But soon something magical happened: colours effortlessly spilled from her brush, giving life to a mesmerising portrait of the man with brilliant green eyes.

34

The sun sank low on the horizon, casting the sky in a glorious blaze of oranges, pinks and reds. Tipu, now a big boy, lay at Lucy's feet, relishing a bone between his jaws. The cheerful chirping of birds echoed through the air and accompanied Lucy's deft brushstrokes. This would be the last in her series, which she planned to exhibit some day to an audience.

Her eyes swept across the canvas, examining every curve and contour, as she sought perfection in her work. But despite her meticulous endeavours, a sense of unease gnawed at her—a persistent, disquieting suspicion that the soulful depths of the subject's eyes remained beyond her creative reach.

As her hands moved, Lucy found herself assailed by shards of memory—recollections of moments spent with the protagonist of her paintings, the enigmatic djinn. She occasionally wondered if this ethereal being was merely a symbolic manifestation of her own mind, a reflection of her deep-seated desire for a saviour.

She delved deeper into the djinn's confusing persona through her paintings, trying to discover the hidden essence of Iblis, a soul forever adrift in the infinite expanse of time and ceaselessly searching for the comforting warmth of love.

In several of her paintings, Lucy had captured the same tale of the women who had been taken away by death and then rescued by the magical being. The memories seemed to reside within her very fingertips, though she never understood where those inspirations came from.

'Lucy … there is someone for you at the door,' Jancy chechi screamed from the veranda. Tipu stood up from her side and started barking.

'Ask them to come another day, I am a little busy,' she replied without taking her eyes off the painting.

'I asked him to come in, he seems like a gentleman,' Jancy chechi yelled back. 'He says you know him from a lamp business.'

'Lamp business?'

'Yes. Lamp business.'

Lucy's face lit up; a smile stretched across her face. Without a second thought, she dropped everything she held and dashed back to the main house. She darted through the veranda, into the kitchen and then the hall, her heart hammering in anticipation. *Could it be? Had Iblis finally returned?*

In the hall sat a man donning blue jeans and a white T-shirt. Sporting dark brown sunglasses and brandishing a walking cane, he leisurely savoured the laddus and jalebis Jancy chechi had arranged on the table. Even from a distance, Lucy could recognise him instantly. He was the one she had been waiting for: Iblis, her djinn.

'How've you been, Lucy? Did you forget me?' he inquired as soon as she entered the room.

'Where have you been all this time?' she couldn't help but grumble.

'I've been searching for you, Lucy, just as much as you've been searching for me. Being blind doesn't make it easier.'

'Blind?'

'A perpetual night shrouds my vision, blinding me to the grandeur of the world and its many wonders.' He removed his sunglasses, revealing lifeless, pallid eyes.

'What happened?' Lucy stammered. She was taken aback. 'You're the great djinn, the one with all the magic. Can't you heal yourself?'

'Oh, it's nothing. I granted a wish that should've remained unfulfilled, which led to a minor clash with Death,' he explained, replacing his sunglasses and resuming his enjoyment of the snacks. 'As long as I am bound to the lamp, I must obey its rules.'

'Did all this happen because of me?' she inquired.

Her thoughts went back to that day: water engulfing the car, the sensation of drowning and the final bubbles of air escaping through her nose. She had thought of him, and he had arrived just in time. 'Lucy, we don't have much time. Make a wish,' he had urged. But she couldn't say a word.

As the water invaded her lungs, a searing pain accompanied her suffocation. She longed for death to release her from this torment. Suddenly, she was weightless, her spirit liberated from her body. 'Come with me, I will keep you safe. The portal to other realms will open soon, we must leave before that,' she faintly recalled Iblis saying as he waited for her under water.

Then, he had cradled her in his arms and whisked her away to a world he had crafted within the lamp.

During that journey, from the water to the world unknown, the djinn's thoughts intertwined with hers, allowing her to understand his intentions. He sought to hide her from Death until her body could be discovered and brought to a hospital, giving her a second chance at life. She also sensed the fear he had experienced, aware that his actions would lead to him losing his sight.

'Oh, the wild and crazy things we'll do, to prove our heart's true content,' Iblis started humming in a humorous tune. His voice brought her back to the present moment. 'Though sight eludes me, dear Lucy, I still see it. For in your mind, I find my sight.'

'Can't I wish you back to vision?' Lucy asked.

'No more wishes, Lucy. No more magic. Without my eyes, I am a nobody.'

'Molae, will he be staying for dinner? Should I fry some karimen and make extra rice?' Janchy chechi had showed up from nowhere.

'Oh, the chef extraordinaire.' Iblis stood up and sniffed in the direction of the person that just entered the room. 'My taste buds are dancing in anticipation of your cooking. Fry all that you have. I want to eat everything.'

Should I put a new mattress cover in the guest bedroom? This man may stay the night. But who is he? Janchy chechi's thoughts echoed in the room. Lucy could hear her clearly as if she had spoken out loud.

'He will be staying for a while, so maybe fix the mattress covers in the other room.' She looked at Jancy chechi who opened her mouth in surprise.

35

That night Lucy had a dream. She was back to the world within the lamp. The ground, as unyielding as she remembered, now bore wider chasms from which searing magma surged forth. The sweltering heat and pungent scent of molten metal threatened to overwhelm her.

In the distance, she spotted Iblis seated beside his crystal ball. But he had transformed. His human guise had vanished entirely and had been replaced by a crimson beast with spiralling horns. Seated upon the throne, it wailed in anguish as its clawed hand shielded its eyes from the glaring light.

Lucy approached the enigmatic figure and peered over his shoulder to catch a glimpse of the crystal ball. In stark contrast to her previous encounter, the sphere emitted no brilliance or beauty. Instead, it exuded a dark aura as it swirled with indistinct, energetic human figures. Each figure moved in a unique hue—some were pure light, others a blend of grey, blue and red. Entranced, Lucy's gaze continued staring at the mysterious display and she found herself consumed by the ball's bewitching gloom.

Abruptly, Lucy found herself walking through a strange, dark version of the human world. She could discern the sounds and smells of those in her vicinity, but the human faces were a blur. The only thing that made them different was the way their bodies were illuminated. She sensed their thoughts emanating from their souls, casting a distinct aura around each individual. With unspoken clarity, Lucy realised that this was the world as perceived by the djinn. This is how he found her again after losing his sight.

Navigating the lightless world proved more challenging than Lucy had anticipated. The inability to see others was disturbing, but the ceaseless undercurrent of anxiety proved far more unsettling. It felt as though danger constantly lurked nearby.

The darkness occasionally lured her thoughts away from the faceless humans before her and towards negative emotions and past traumas. Staying connected to her surroundings became an increasingly difficult task.

This is unbearable, she thought, attempting to retrace her steps. *How can anyone endure such an existence?*

Through sheer determination and unwavering focus, Lucy finally managed to return to the creature occupying the throne. 'Is this how you spend your days now, my dear djinn?' She placed her hands on his face, her heart heavy with sorrow.

'Why don't you want me to make a wish to cure your sight? What are you thinking, Iblis?' Lucy inquired, embracing him without hesitation. And without her knowing, this simple gesture set them on another journey deep into Iblis's mind.

A djinn's subconscious is an endlessly intricate maze. It's a place where his thoughts, motives and emotions search of a refuge. Lucy soon found herself in its midst, lost and disoriented. Ghostly images of his past unfolded around her.

As if the place already knew what Lucy was after, a specific memory began to unfurl before her eyes.

Iblis stood in a magical circle in the middle of a pentagram. Human skulls were placed on the intricate design that was drawn with human blood. Five sorcerers stood on the five ends of the star, chanting ancient Egyptian spells. With each recital, their voices rose. Iblis felt like his power was leaving his body. He was barely able to stand straight. He fell to his knees and started screaming in protest.

'How dare you try to seal the king of djinns?' His growls echoed in the room. 'I will throw your flesh and bones to the demons of the underworld; I will burn down your city and people ...'

The chanting in the room grew louder. The djinn started losing more of his sight and sense of smell. He started shapeshifting into a man, to a bird, to an animal. He finally ended up in his demonic form with two horns. The growls continued.

'You can't escape the ancient magic, old djinn. I have your name—Iblis, Iblis, Iblis.' Senenmut, Hatshepsut's new lover, entered the room with a lamp that had an eerie glow. 'No matter how powerful you are, you will follow the lamp's rules and spend an eternity in solitude. You would be a slave to this lamp, and you will do as it asks of you.'

Iblis cast a quick look at the engraved scriptures on the lamp's metal surface as they slowly came off and made their way into the magical circle. Like a shadowy serpent, it coiled around Iblis's body and pulled him into the lamp.

'Listen carefully, Iblis. You're no longer free to wander. Your new home is where I sit, and your magic is only to be used upon your master's request. Disobey, and you'll lose a piece of your soul and body. Your path to freedom is to serve a human and grant them three wishes. But remember, even freedom comes at a price. Once you're released, you'll return to your realm with no memory of what has passed. You won't seek revenge from those who have done you wrong.' The lamp that entrapped him also revealed its rules. The djinn's anguished howls followed; their intensity caused Lucy's ears to throb with pain.

36

'Never trust a blind djinn.'

Lucy stayed awake in her bed the whole morning. She was upset even though she was in love again. She had never felt such intense feelings—that too for someone so unexpected. She couldn't even bring herself to think certain things because those thoughts were just strange. Falling in love with a djinn was one such thing. It felt more weird than exciting.

She thought about the first time they met in that hotel room. The tall blue creature that she initially dismissed as unreal had become the most important being for her. *How strange can life get?*

Amidst the bizarre events and altered pasts and futures, Lucy might have continued to believe her experiences were mere fairy tales, had it not been for Jancy chechi's confirmation of Iblis's existence. However, as she got more and more attached to Iblis, she found herself grappling with a growing sense of desperation rather than fulfilment—an unsettling fear that she would lose the love she had discovered just as it had begun to blossom.

Iblis, now a mere shadow of his former self, blind and powerless, looked like a lost pet without a home. Within his vulnerability, Lucy felt a degree of control over him, as if he had come down from his high place, allowing her to truly see his essence.

In a transient moment, she attempted to weigh her burgeoning love for him against the sorrow he bore for his vanished sight. She knew this wasn't fair, but she could not resist deeming it justifiable for her own heart's sake.

What is love, truly? Is it not clinging to someone, even when we know they may find solace far from our embrace?

As she confronted the stark realities of life, her own insecurities weighed on her—the impending return of loneliness and the inevitable search for companionship that would follow. *Great sacrifices are not for those who fear tomorrow, not for those uncertain of their next move or those unsure of whom to confide in.* She wasn't ready to play the martyr, the sacrificial lamb, to release her love for a nobler cause. She had tasted the bitter pill of being left behind by a loved one and harboured no desire to experience it again.

Beyond the room, Lucy heard Tipu's exuberant yaps—those innocent, high-pitched barks that spoke of joy. Even with closed eyes, she could sense that the pup was playing with Iblis in the garden. And with a slight change of focus, she connected with both of them, sensing the way they felt about each other. *Is this love? Is this the sensation everyone seeks—being wholly selfless and caring for another in each passing moment?*

Lucy drew a deep breath and braced herself to delve into the deepest depths of her innermost longing. Her mind extended beyond the confines of her surroundings, journeying across the dew-kissed grass, the blossoms and the minuscule droplets upon them, seeking to connect with the duo's thoughts. Somehow, she had mastered the art of tuning into others. She had become the vessel of magic.

First, she connected to her dog. She could feel love and loyalty radiating from him, and it gave her comfort. The animal's initial fear of Iblis had turned into trust. He was enjoying playing with the stranger, chasing after balls tossed into the distance. Then she moved her focus to Iblis. When she tried connecting to his mind, she felt only silence and a grim sensation of loneliness.

While his body appeared to play with the dog, his thoughts were in turmoil. Different parts of his mind battled—some advised him to draw upon his inner wisdom to find solace, others urged him to deceive the human woman to escape the unrelenting darkness.

'You have all that you need, King. You have found the love you searched for, she is the one. The kindest of them all,' a tranquil voice emerged. 'What of your throne? You are the king of djinns, Iblis, don't forget that,' another voice countered. 'How can someone live in this darkness? Isn't this an eternal punishment?' Now the voices had started to overlap. 'Love, Iblis, is the soul's eternal quest. You, of all beings, understand this better than anyone. Why lose the very thing you've searched for for so long?'

As the chaos of voices engulfed the djinn, he felt lost in the complex corners of his mind. His consciousness drifted away from the world his body inhabited, carrying Lucy along like a paper boat caught in a downpour.

The deeper they ventured, the more challenging it became to maintain a connection with the reality they had left behind. Iblis thought of his time on the throne; he had been the almighty, the one who controlled a realm with a mere whisper. He felt as though such a destiny had been etched into his being since the dawn of time; it was an overwhelming purpose that had defined his very existence. The seductive potency of that power called to him, like an irresistible siren urging him to seize what was once his own.

'You are the king, the one true king of djinns. What are you doing with these puny humans in a world forsaken?' The voices in his mind remerged. 'Trick her into making a wish and come back to where you truly belong,' another commented.

'Iblis, remember the emptiness and loneliness that consumed you on that throne. No amount of control or power could fill the void within you. Why else would you have constantly looked at the humans through your crystal ball?' The voices continued their impassioned debate. 'The power, don't you yearn for it? When did you become so weak?'

Iblis started losing control of himself, succumbing to the primal instincts that lurked within his demonic nature.

Soon, he became disoriented, unable to discern his identity within the unending darkness. *Where was I before these thoughts assailed me? Where am I within this vast, lightless universe?* Like a feral creature reverting to its primitive form in the face of danger, the djinn's nails extended from his fingertips. His face contorted into something monstrous and he readied himself to annihilate anything that crossed his path.

Lucy sprang from her bed and dashed towards the garden. On her way, she heard Tipu's distressed growling, a desperate plea for help.

37

In the garden, Lucy was confronted by a horrifying sight. A massive, four-legged serpent with three distinct animal heads towered over the cowering Tipu. It emitted a deafening screech before lunging at the dog.

Sensing the imminent danger, the dog leaped to one side. But the djinn anticipated his movements and cornered Tipu against a wall. With the animal trapped, the djinn opened its three mouths wide, unveiling a long, writhing tongue, saliva dripping from its edges. The tongue coiled around the frightened pup, preparing to drag it into the creature's gaping maws.

'Iblis … Iblis … stop!' Lucy screamed from a distance.

As her words reached the monstrous being, its frenzied movements slowed, eventually coming to a halt. It turned around and sniffed the air. 'Lucy, is that you? Where is this place?' it inquired. 'Am I still on Earth?' Then, unable to make sense of anything, the creature collapsed to the ground.

'It's me, Iblis, you have nothing to worry about,' Lucy assured him as she raced to his side, wrapping her arms around his neck.

'I don't know what's happening to me, Lucy. Without my eyes, I'm losing track of time and space. I am dying', the djinn sobbed. His body, like malleable clay, shifted through various forms—from a snake, a bird, a dog, to finally a human—before becoming still. 'But I will overcome them. I can do that for you. You are my Lucy. And I love you.'

As if the sight before her had wrought a seismic shift within her and melted her ego, Lucy spoke those words—the words she loathed to utter yet knew deep down were the right thing to say. It wasn't easy by any means; as the words left her lips, her eyes brimmed with tears and she felt a host of emotions. But she understood that without this sacrifice, Iblis would never survive. She had come to know his heart and soul as intimately as her own, and in that moment she chose to bear the unbearable pain for his salvation.

'I wish, I wish, my dear djinn, for you to be set free from the lamp and return to the world where you truly belong. With all my heart, I fervently hope that you will not forget me, and that one day, when you have reclaimed your true self, you will come back to see me,' Lucy cried out loud.

The lamp, resting amongst assorted curios on the crystalline display in the hallway, began to tremble. At first, it was a subtle vibration, like the whispers of a distant earthquake. But within seconds, it intensified, clanging against the frosty glass of the cabinet with a resonant clamour that echoed throughout the room.

Janchy chechi, who was sweeping the floor, paused. Her attention was drawn to the spectacle of the lamp now shaking with a near-violent vigour.

The once smooth, polished surface of the lamp became rough, the gleaming bronze dulled into a murky, ancient patina. The ornate engravings, which had once chronicled the story of the djinn's imprisonment, seemed to come alive, writhing and twisting as though trying to break free from the confines of the metal. The air around the lamp crackled with electricity, and the temperature in the room began to rise.

'Molae, molae, something is happening here!' Janchy chechi shouted, standing stunned in front of the cabinet.

The metal shrieked and groaned, the stress of its transformations pushing it to the brink of collapse. With one final, cataclysmic shudder, the lamp exploded, sending shards of twisted metal and molten bronze hurtling through the air. The force of the blast knocked the woman off her feet, causing the windows to shatter explosively.

Outside, Iblis's form ascended gracefully into the air. For a second, he was suspended in a moment of ethereal beauty. Slowly, his body began to disintegrate, metamorphosing into a luminous torrent of golden dust. Whisked away by the tender embrace of the wandering zephyr, he disappeared without getting the chance to share a parting word, leaving an indelible mark on the spirit of the one who had granted him his freedom.

38

Three years later.

The vivacious buzz of the Kochi Biennale filled the air. It was a refreshing antidote to the ceaseless roar of vehicles on the street. The sun cast a warm, golden glow over the historic city of Kochi, illuminating its Portuguese architecture and charming streets that served as the perfect canvas for this celebration of artistic expression.

Visitors, a diverse mix of art enthusiasts, curious onlookers and teenagers, converged upon the sprawling exhibition grounds with paper cones filled with fried groundnut. The scent of street food vendors tantalised their senses, while a group of musicians strummed their instruments nearby, providing a rhythmic soundtrack to the unfolding scene.

Upon entering the main exhibition hall, the atmosphere shifted to one of reverent appreciation. Subdued whispers of the visitors echoed through the room and served as a tribute to the awe-inspiring artwork that adorned the white walls. Twelve captivating paintings hung in perfect harmony, each piece a part of a narrative meticulously woven by their artist, Lucy.

The paintings varied in size and orientation, with some standing tall while others embraced the breadth of the wall. Despite their differences, a unifying theme emerged—a mesmerising interplay of composition and colour that bound them together in an exquisite visual treat.

Next to them, a polished wooden board offered a glimpse into the mind of the artist. 'Lucy and the Djinn' it said in bold letters. The words below spoke of her passion for exploring the deepest recesses of human emotion and the transcendent power of art to connect us all. She briefly talked about lost love and how it can bring out the best in each of us.

Lucy patiently answered the visitors' questions about the meaning and symbolism behind her paintings.

'… the blue tone,' she continued, her voice soft, 'describes melancholia, the bittersweet symphony of longing that etches itself upon our hearts.

'The vibrant hues that ripple across the canvas embody the emotions we experience in the throes of love—confusion, fear, anxiety and euphoria.

'The patterns you see,' she explained, her eyes gleaming with intensity, 'are a reflection of the emotions that entwined two souls. A dance of love and loss, of connection and separation, plays out in the subtle interplay of colour and form.'

'What about the large human-like creature in all the paintings? Is that symbolic?' a man from the crowd asked. Lucy's eyes sparkled as she pondered the question. Not a day had passed without thoughts of Iblis crossing her mind, yet the question took her back to the day he disappeared without a word. Her heart felt heavy.

'That, you see,' her fingers absentmindedly raking through her hair, her voice barely audible, 'is the embodiment of love's elusive nature.'

The crowd leaned in.

'Our souls, ever wandering in search of love's sweet nectar, sometimes takes us to the very edge of our existence. It might not always be as soft and sweet as we might imagine. To love is to unveil the depths of our being, to bare our hearts not just to the promise of joy but also to the possibility of loss.' Her gaze held the audience captive.

'To lose love,' she whispered, 'is like losing oneself. But it is only in the midst of that pain that we can understand that life itself is a dance of love and its absence. It is an eternal waltz that guides our steps towards self-discovery and growth.'

Though most of the audience did not understand half of what she said, some immediately began to applaud. Then there was a moment of silence, and the visitors gradually dispersed.

Lucy sat on the chair next to one of her paintings. It had been a while since she felt the weight of her memories. For a split second, she was back in her past, at a time when she was confused and lost, fighting her imaginary problems. She had come a long way.

'Life is good, it is good!' she whispered softly, before walking close to the final painting in the series—a wide canvas illustrating a dying djinn cradled in a girl's lap, a shattered lamp at their feet. She studied his eyes, wondering if she had managed to get them right, at least this time. *Oh, Iblis, how I miss you.*

'So, it is a tale of love's fleeting beauty, of souls torn apart. I have to say, it's beautiful,' someone greeted her from behind. Lucy nodded and replied, 'Thank you.'

'I wonder if this is the end or if there's more to the story,' the voice continued.

'What?' She turned around. The man was wearing blue jeans and a hoodie.

'You heard me right, Lucy. I wonder if it's the end or a new beginning,' he grinned.

Lucy's gaze met his intense, emerald eyes and she smiled.